Dear Reader,

When I first started to write, my favorite reading was sagas, stories spanning not just generations but centuries, with young brides who grew to become loved matriarchs, aggravating younger sons who matured into fine strong men, and daughters who, like their mothers, kept a watchful maternal eye on their children—and their children's children.

As an author, I have concentrated on the modern-day romances I enjoy writing so much. But the desire to write a series of novels based around one family has never left me—partly because my own personal ideal is to live in a small country town surrounded by a network of family connections. And I am fortunate to live in a part of the English countryside, Cheshire, which is steeped in history, the perfect setting for my family series.

I very much wanted to write about the emotion, joy and often sadness that bond a family together, and with this series I feel that I have in some sense fulfilled a part of myself—the name Crighton originally belonged to my husband's mother's family. I hope you will take my fictional family to your heart and love them as much as I do.

Penny Jordan

Welcome to Penny Jordan's miniseries featuring the Crighton family.

This is no ordinary family because, although the affluent Crightons might appear to have it all, shocking revelations and heartache lie just beneath the surface of their perfect, charmed lives.

Penny Jordan has been writing for more than fifteen years and has an outstanding record: over 100 novels published, including the phenomenally successful **Power Games, Cruel Legacy** and **Power Play,** which hit the *New York Times* and *Sunday Times* bestseller lists.

Her latest mainstream release— **A Perfect Family**—gives the full inside story of the Crighton family and is available through MIRA Books. Their story continues in three Harlequin Presents novels:

The Perfect Seduction (#1941 March 1998)
Perfect Marriage Material (#1948 April 1998)
The Perfect Match? (#1954 May 1998)

Penny Jordan

The Perfect Seduction

Harlequin Books

TORONTO • NEW YORK • LONDON
AMSTERDAM • PARIS • SYDNEY • HAMBURG
STOCKHOLM • ATHENS • TOKYO • MILAN
MADRID • WARSAW • BUDAPEST • AUCKLAND

ISBN 0-373-11941-0

THE PERFECT SEDUCTION

First North American Publication 1998.

The Crighton Family

BEN CRIGHTON: Proud patriarch of the family, a strong-minded character in his seventies, determined to see his dynasty thrive and prosper.

RUTH CRIGHTON: Ben's sister. After a tragic love affair during the war years, Ruth has devoted herself to the family and become a source of comfort and advice.

DAVID CRIGHTON: Twin brother of Jon, and favorite son of Ben. Glamorous, charming and selfish, he doesn't deserve his status as heir to the Crighton fortune....

TIGGY CRIGHTON: Beautiful, fragile wife of David, an ex-model who is determined to remain youthful as long as possible. Desperate for attention, she flirts with all men.

OLIVIA JOHNSON: Daughter of David and Tiggy, an independent young woman who's met her match in husband Caspar. In defiance of family opposition, Livvy became a talented lawyer outside the family firm.

CASPAR JOHNSON: An American law tutor, devoted to his wife, Olivia.

JON CRIGHTON: Younger twin of David, steady and reliable, he carries the burden of responsibility in the family law firm.

JENNY CRIGHTON: Wife of Jon, a very practical and warmhearted woman devoted to her family. Partner in a local antique business and a role model for her niece, Livvy.

LOUISE and KATE: Twin teenage daughters of Jon and Jenny. Vibrant, spirited characters determined to go their own way.

JOSS: Charming ten-year-old son of Jon and Jenny.

LUKE CRIGHTON: Charismatic, devastatingly attractive, a talented lawyer with women vying for his attention. Part of the Chester branch of the Crighton family.

BOBBIE MILLER: A beautiful and bright young woman, determined to have revenge on the Crighton family for the heartache they caused her mother. She sees Luke as a means of getting close to the family....

SAM MILLER: Bobbie's twin sister, living in America.

The Crighton Family

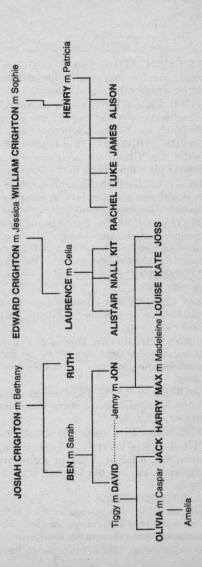

Haslewich branch of the family

Chester branch of the family

JOSIAH CRIGHTON m Bethany

EDWARD CRIGHTON m Jessica   WILLIAM CRIGHTON m Sophie

HENRY m Patricia

LAURENCE m Celia

RACHEL LUKE JAMES ALISON

ALISTAIR NIALL KIT

BEN m Sarah   RUTH

Jenny m JON

Tiggy m Caspar JACK HARRY MAX m Madeleine LOUISE KATE JOSS

OLIVIA m Caspar DAVID

Amelia

CHAPTER ONE

Joss saw her first. He was on his way back from visiting his great-aunt Ruth in her house on Church Walk and *she* was standing in the churchyard studying the headstones, her head bent over one of them, a tumble of thick, glossy blonde curls obscuring her face. When she looked up, alerted to his presence by the sound of a small twig cracking under his foot, Joss stared at her in open wonder and awe.

She was tall, much much taller than him; at least six foot, he estimated.

'And a couple of inches,' she drawled in amusement as she watched the way he was assessing her height, 'and then I guess you'd be somewhere roundabouts right. I guess no one kinda likes to think of a woman being over six foot. Tell them you're five-eleven, it's okay and my, aren't you lucky being so tall, but tell them you're six-one going on six-two and they think you're a freak. After all, what kinda right-thinking woman allows herself to grow too tall for most of your average guys.'

'I don't think you're too tall,' Joss told her gallantly, manfully squaring his own ten-year-old shoulders and looking up into her eyes.

And what eyes they were, surely the deepest, darkest blue that ever was. Joss had never seen eyes like them before. He had never seen anyone like *her* before.

She watched him gravely for a second before her mouth curled into a smile that made Joss's insides turn to jelly and told him, 'Why that's mighty kind of you, but I guess I know what you're really thinking...that for a woman this tall finding a boy tall enough for me to look up to is kinda hard. Yes, well, you're right,' she went on with another dazzling smile, 'and if you happen to know of any—'.

'I do,' Joss told her quickly, already fiercely protective of her; already determined that no one should dare to criticise her or find her less than complete perfection, not even she herself. As he gazed at her, his eyes mirrored the intensity and immediacy of his first calf-love.

Speculatively she hesitated, not wanting to hurt him and yet at the same time wary of any involvement that might deflect her from her purpose in being there.

Haslewich might not be on any official tourist route like Chester, but she had been determined to visit it and, as yet, she had still not seen the remains of the castle and its wall, nor the newly sanitised salt-works that had recently been opened to the public as a tourist attraction, never mind the rest of the town's historic sites. So far, in fact, all she had done was glance around the church-yard.

'I've got two cousins,' she heard Joss telling her. 'Well, they aren't exactly cousins,' he acknowledged. 'They're really seconds, or maybe even thirds, I don't know which. Aunt Ruth would know.

'But anyway, James is six foot two and Luke is even taller and then there's Alistair and Niall and Kit and Saul, too, I suppose, although he's quite old—'

'Gee…I'm really impressed,' Bobbie interrupted him gently.

'I could always introduce you to them,' Joss offered enthusiastically. 'That is, if you're going to be here for a while…?'

He let the question hang.

'Well, that kinda depends. You see…gee…I'm sorry but I don't know your name. We haven't introduced our-selves yet, have we? I'm Bobbie, short for Roberta,' she told him whilst inwardly acknowledging ruefully that she really didn't have the time to waste on this sort of thing, but he was just so appealing and not a day over ten or eleven. Give him another ten or fifteen years and he was going to be dynamite. She wondered absently what his cousins were actually like.

'Bobbie...I like that,' he told her and she hid her smile as the look in his eyes told her that whatever her name had turned out to be, it would have got an equally enthusiastic response. 'I'm Joss,' he added, 'Joss Crighton.'

Joss Crighton. That altered everything. Thick eyelashes veiled her eyes.

'Well now, Joss Crighton, suppose you and I go find a diner and get to know one another a little bit better and you can tell me all about these cousins of yours. Would they be Crightons, too?' she asked him casually.

'Yes, they are,' he agreed. 'But...well, it's a long story.'

'I can't wait to hear it. They're my favourite kind,' she assured him solemnly.

As he fell into step beside her, matching his own stride to her long-legged, elegantly feminine walk, Joss couldn't help stealing awed glances at her.

She was wearing cream trousers and a shirt in the same colour with a camelly-coloured coat over the top; her blonde hair, now that she had lifted her head, hung down past her shoulders in thick, luxurious waves. Joss could feel his heart threatening to burst with pride and delight as he guided her through the town square and into one of the pretty, narrow streets that led off it.

'Gee, is that really real?' she paused to enquire as they passed a clutch of half-timbered Elizabethan buildings, huddled together for support.

'Yes, they were built in the reign of Elizabeth I,' Joss told her importantly. 'The main structure of wooden beams is infilled with panels of wattle and daub—that's sort of bits of branches held together with a mixture of straw, mud and other things,' he told her kindly.

'Uh-huh,' Bobbie responded, refraining from telling him that she had majored in British history before switching her talents to a more modern and financially rewarding field.

'We don't actually have diners in this country,' Joss informed her politely, 'but there is a...a place just down here....'

Bobbie hid her amusement. No doubt he was taking her to the town's McDonald's. Only, as she soon discovered, he wasn't and she hesitated fractionally as he directed her attention to a very smart and up-market-looking wine bar, glancing thoughtfully from the sign above the doorway that stipulated that alcoholic beverages were not supplied to persons under eighteen to Joss's very obviously nowhere near eighteen-year-old face and back again. She didn't want to hurt his dignity, but at the same time she didn't exactly relish the thought of being asked to leave because she was accompanied by a minor.

'I can go in so long as I don't have anything alcoholic to drink. I know the people who run it,' he explained as he pushed the door open for her. At the same time he crossed his fingers behind his back as he tried to calculate just what he could buy with what was left of his week's bus fare and spending money, which was all he had in his pocket, and whether or not Minnie Cooke, who ran the wine bar, would give him any credit.

Minnie's brother, Guy, was in partnership with Joss's mother in an antique business, which they ran. She recognised Joss as soon as he walked into the wine bar, her eyebrows lifting slightly as she looked from Joss to his companion.

'Yes, Joss?' she asked him cautiously.

'I...er...we'd both like a drink and something to eat,'

he told her firmly, adding in a far less certain voice, 'Minnie, could I have a word with you?'

'Look, why don't you let me make this my treat?' Bobbie offered, guessing his dilemma. He was just at an age when any kind of public humiliation, no matter how slight, was a major issue, and the last thing she wanted to do was to hurt or slight him in any way, but Minnie Cooke, too, had summed up the situation and stepped into the breach.

'Why don't you find yourselves a table. I'll send someone over to take your order. We can sort out the bill later,' she added to Joss quietly, as Bobbie made her way to a table.

Whoever Joss's companion was, she certainly was a stunningly beautiful woman, Minnie acknowledged as she dispatched one of her many nieces to take their order. She was most probably a guest they had staying with the family. Olivia, Joss's cousin, was married to that American, wasn't she?

'Jade,' she told her niece sharply, 'go and serve table four.'

'I'll have a glass of Perrier with lemon and ice,' Bobbie told Jade easily. 'Nothing to eat, though.'

'I'll have the same.' Joss couldn't quite conceal his relief as he heard Bobbie order, beaming his approval at her across their shared table.

'So,' she prompted after Jade had brought them their drinks. 'These cousins of yours.' She put her elbow on the table and leaned her chin on her hand as she smiled at him.

Joss was completely bewitched. A huge lump filled his throat and he had the same indescribable feeling that he always got when he watched the young badger or fox cubs coming out for their first night's play in the spring, watched over by their mothers. Like them, she touched his emotions in a way he simply didn't have the words to describe.

Guiltily Bobbie nibbled on her bottom lip. She really ought not to be doing this. He was so young and so vulnerable. She was here for a purpose, she reminded herself sternly, and she couldn't let herself be swayed from that self-chosen task now, especially not by...

'I guess with their kinda height they must be sports jocks, huh,' she joked to Joss as she banished her unwanted thoughts.

'No,' Joss told her seriously.

He couldn't take his eyes off her; he had never seen anyone remotely like her. There couldn't *be* anyone like her. She was unique, wonderful, perfect and certainly nothing like his own twin sisters or the other girls he knew. She was older than them, of course, just how much older he wasn't quite sure but she must be twenty-something.

'Luke and James are both barristers,' he told her. 'That is, they're...' He tried to think of the American term, suddenly realising that she might not fully understand just what a barrister was.

But apparently she did, because she shook her head and told him firmly, 'Yes, I know...lawyers, huh. Gee. I guess I'd have preferred it if they *were* sports jocks,' she confessed, wrinkling her nose.

'Well, they are, sort of,' Joss assured her. 'James played rugger for his school and so did Luke and Luke was an Oxford Blue, as well. That's...that's with rowing,' he explained.

'Rowing...' Bobbie just managed to conceal her smile. When she had been doing her master's, there had been a couple of guys over from Oxbridge working alongside her. 'And you're sure that they're as tall as you say they are?' she teased him mock-seriously.

Joss nodded his head.

'And they're really your cousins...?'

'Third cousins, I think,' Joss agreed.

'Third cousins... Gee...I guess you'd better explain to me what that means,' Bobbie coaxed him, mentally silencing the scornful inner voice that demanded to know why she needed to ask that question when she had a whole string of thirds and fourths of her own back home.

'Well, I'm not sure exactly what it means,' Joss began, 'but you see in the beginning there was Great-Grandfather Josiah. He came from Chester with his wife to start a new solicitor's practice here in Haslewich because of a quarrel he had had with his father and brothers in Chester and so the Crighton family here in Haslewich is separate from the Crightons who live in Chester, but we are still related. Luke and James and their sisters, Alison and Rachel, as well as Alistair, Niall and Kit all belong to the Chester branch of the family. Luke's father, Henry, and his brother, Laurence, are both barristers, too, or at least they were. They're now both retired. Luke is a QC, that's Queen's Counsel. That's what Gramps wants Max to be, but I'm not sure—'

'Whoa, hang on...hang on.' Bobbie laughed. 'Who are Gramps and Max? It's all just too confusing...' She shook her head.

'It wouldn't be,' Joss assured her with great daring, 'if you met them.'

'Met them?' Bobbie's dense blue eyes widened in curiosity. 'Well now, there's a thought, but—'

'We...my twin sisters are having a party this weekend to celebrate their eighteenth birthdays,' Joss hurried on eagerly. 'It's going to be held at the Grosvenor...that's a hotel in Chester. You could come and then you could meet them all....'

'*I* could come...' Bobbie frowned. 'Well now, Joss, that's mighty kind of you, but I don't think...'

'You could come as *my* friend,' Joss told her. 'It's allowed...I am allowed to take a friend. It will be all right....'

A friend maybe, Bobbie conceded but she doubted that the type of friend his parents had in mind when making such an agreement was a twenty-six-year-old woman they didn't know, especially when... Joss was watching her...waiting, a look of mingled pleading and hope in his eyes, and she didn't have the heart to disappoint him, and besides...why look a gift horse in the mouth after all...?

'And I'll get to meet these tall cousins of yours, you say?' she responded, pretending to be weighing the matter up.

Joss nodded his head.

'And you think he'll like me, do you, this Luke? Wasn't that who you said was the taller of the two?'

'Well, er...' Suddenly Joss was flushing and unable to meet her eyes.

'What is it?' she quizzed him. 'Doesn't he like blondes?'

'Oh yes, he does,' Joss assured her fervently, immediately looking so mortified that she had to fight hard not to explode into laughter as she guessed what was wrong.

'Ah...he likes blondes, but not great tall ones, is that it?' she enquired gently. 'He's the type who prefers them small and shrimp-sized to match the size of his own brain. Poor guy, I guess it's not his fault that he has such poor taste. So I guess I'll just have to concentrate on James, won't I? It's all right,' she told Joss with a kind smile. 'When a girl gets to be my height she kinda learns not to be too fussy.'

'James is very nice,' Joss assured her.

'But Luke's the number-one guy, right?' Bobbie guessed.

Joss paused judiciously for a moment before pronouncing, 'James is more easygoing than Luke. He doesn't... Luke always notices everything, even when you think he hasn't, and then he—'

'He lets you know about it, right?' Bobbie offered shrewdly. 'I guess he's the domineering type, a control freak.' She wrinkled her deliciously shaped nose, her mouth curling into a slightly cynical smile. 'I kinda think of the two of them, I'd definitely prefer James and—'

'No...no, you wouldn't,' Joss felt bound to tell her. 'You see, girls like Luke,' he explained carefully and then added, 'Olivia, she's my real cousin and she's married to an American. She says Luke's a real-life personification of a tall, dark and handsome grade A male with just a hint of brooding sexuality thrown in and that it's no wonder he can have his pick of the female population.'

'He sounds a real wow,' Bobbie muttered grimly.

Joss gave her an uncertain look before offering helpfully, 'Olivia says that he would be an awful lot happier if he was either less spectacularly sexy or less intelligent.'

As she digested this comment before making any response, Bobbie reflected inwardly that Olivia, whoever she was, would probably be discomfited to realise that her comment, which had obviously been intended for an adult audience, had been overheard by Joss's perceptive young ears.

'Beauty *and* brains,' she marvelled in a sweetly derisive voice whilst keeping these thoughts to herself. 'Looks like I'm going to have some competition. Perhaps I'd better go for the other one after all.'

Joss pondered the matter. 'Well, if you come with me to the twins' birthday party, you'll be able to see them both,' he suggested winningly.

For a second, Bobbie hesitated, her natural essential kindness and honesty overcoming the determination that had brought her so many thousands of miles. It wasn't really fair to use Joss, who was quite plainly innocent of any guile or self-seeking in what quite possibly could turn out to be a very messy situation indeed, but if she didn't... His unexpected invitation offered her a short cut that was really too generous a gift of fate for her to ignore and besides...

'You are still coming, aren't you?' Joss pressed her anxiously. Still?

'Well, I'd like to,' Bobbie agreed, 'but are you sure your family won't—'

'Mum's already said that I can bring a friend and it's a buffet meal and not a sit-down thing and there'll be plenty to eat and...'

Almost tripping over his words in his haste to get them out, Joss raced on, whilst Bobbie listened chin in hand and hid a small, rueful smile. He really was very young.

'And it's at a hotel in Chester, this party...?'

'Yes, the Grosvenor, you'll like it,' Joss assured her. 'It's part owned by the Duke.' His forehead suddenly furrowed. He had a vague awareness that a series of complex arrangements had been made to ferry all the guests to Chester and it struck him that it would hardly be gentlemanly or gallant to suggest that his guest make her way to the hotel on her own, but on the other hand... 'Er...I don't know where you're staying,' he began manfully.

'That's okay,' Bobbie returned easily, immediately understanding his dilemma. 'I know where the Grosvenor is and I can make my own way there.' No need to tell him that she was actually staying in the hotel herself, even if the small deceit, so unfamiliar to her normal openness, did sit uncomfortably on her conscience.

'Oh good, I could meet you in reception,' Joss offered.

'Mum wants us to be there early and the thing isn't due to start until eight so I could meet you then if you like.'

'Eight will be fine with me,' Bobbie assured him.

They had both finished their drinks. Joss checked furtively in his pocket; with luck he would just about have enough money to pay for them.

'Until Saturday, then,' Bobbie told him as they parted company outside the wine bar.

'Until Saturday,' Joss agreed and then flushed as he asked her anxiously, 'You will be there, won't you?'

'You can bet on it,' Bobbie promised him.

Thoughtfully Bobbie made her way back to where she had parked her hire-car. Fate, it seemed, was on her side. Her walking pace increased as she glanced at her watch to check what time it would be back home; there was a phone call she had promised to make.

'James, have you got a moment?'

James looked up as his elder brother walked into his office. In anyone else's company James would automatically have attracted the discreet attention and admiration of the women who saw him. Six foot two with the strong, broad-shouldered body of an ex-Rugby player, he was boyishly handsome in a way that was accentuated by the thick, soft brown hair that flopped over his forehead and the generous warmth of his smile. At thirty-two he looked younger; he was the kind of man who women knew instinctively would be kind to animals, children and old ladies, and inevitably they wanted to mother him.

No woman in her right mind on the young side of forty, and a good many of those over it, felt in the least like mothering Luke.

'I wonder why it is that whenever I think of Luke the word that most easily comes next to mind is lust?' Olivia had once asked James ruefully.

James had simply shaken his head.

There was no doubt that with Luke being almost six foot four and having shoulders even more powerfully broad than his own, the classic Crighton profile with its strong nose and even stronger jaw (which had somehow passed him by), combined with very dark brown almost black hair and smoky grey eyes, had the kind of effect on women that could only be likened to unexpectedly swallowing a strong alcoholic drink. First came the shock of its unexpected power in the nervous system, followed by the lethal combination of dizziness and euphoria linked to a dangerous diminishment of logic and self-control.

And the pity of it was that rather than enjoying the effect he had on the female sex, Luke, whilst not oblivious to it, was certainly dismissively contemptuous of it—and, it had to be said, of the women who reacted to it.

'I wanted to have a word with you about the Marshall case before I leave for Brussels.'

'You haven't forgotten that we've got the Haslewich do on at the Grosvenor this weekend, have you?' James asked him.

Luke shook his head as he perched on the corner of his brother's desk. Both of them were qualified barristers working from the same set of chambers as their father and uncle used to, but it was Luke who was the most senior, having been appointed a Queen's Counsel the previous year, one of the youngest in the country, a fact about which his father had lost no time bragging to his cousin, Ben Crighton, in Haslewich.

Henry and Ben were a generation removed from the original quarrel that had split the Crighton family, but they still continued the subtle interfamily rivalry their fathers had begun, much to Luke's irritation.

He had far more important things to worry about than

outdoing his cousin, Max Crighton, and he had no wish to take up the baton of family competitiveness and run with it even if Max was showing signs of wishing to do so.

'No, I haven't forgotten,' he agreed, 'although I can't say that I'm particularly looking forward to it.'

'Mmm…well, it certainly won't be boring,' James commented. 'Max is coming up from London with his wife.'

'Mmm…' was Luke's only comment.

'He's doing pretty well for himself by all accounts,' James continued. 'He's got a good tenancy, though. You'd be hard put to find a better set of chambers, and—'

'*He's* got a good tenancy?' Luke broke in dryly, emphasising the word 'he's'. 'I rather thought his sudden advancement into the upper echelons of one of London's most prestigious sets of chambers owed more to the efforts of his father-in-law than to Max himself.'

'You've never really liked him, have you?' James asked his brother.

'No, I haven't,' Luke agreed, coldly adding, 'it's hard to think of him as Jon's son. If *David* had been his father…'

'That was an odd business, wasn't it?' James said. 'The way David just upped and left like that after his heart attack, disappearing…'

'Mmm…I dare say he had his reasons,' Luke commented obliquely. He had heard certain rumours about David—none of them ever verified, but he had sensed that despite the strenuous and meticulous efforts that Jon had made to track down his twin brother, he was almost relieved not to have been able to find him.

In Luke's opinion Jon had always been the better one of the pair even if Jon's own father had always shown a public and very marked preference for David. And now

Jon and Jenny's twin daughters were eighteen. God, that made him feel old. He was virtually twice their age, and as his great-aunt Alice had reminded him pugnaciously the last time he had seen her, fast approaching an age where, in her words, he ran the danger of no longer being seen as an eligible bachelor but rather an unpleasant misanthrope.

He knew that he was commonly considered to be aloof and disdainful; that he had the reputation of being overly arrogant, too sure of himself and dismissive of women who made a play for him; that he was, in fact, immune to the vulnerability of falling in love.

Not so. He had once been in love and very, very deeply, or so he had thought at the time, but she had married someone else and lived to regret it. She had told him this when she had come to see him, tears filling her eyes as she confessed that her marriage was over and that she needed his help to find a good divorce lawyer.

'Have you thought long and hard about what you'll be giving up,' he had asked her seriously.

'Of course I have,' she had cried, pushing trembling fingers into her hair as she went on tearfully, 'but do you really think that any of that matters. That his wealth, his title, that any of it means anything when I'm so unhappy…?'

'You married him,' he pointed out bluntly to her.

'Yes,' she had agreed, her mouth trembling as much as her hand had done earlier. 'At eighteen I believed I loved him. At eighteen you can convince yourself of anything you want to believe. He seemed so…'

'So rich,' he offered.

She had given him a hurt look.

'I didn't stop to think. He swept me off my feet. I thought then you should never have let me go, Luke,' she told him quietly.

He paused for a moment before answering her evenly,

'As I remember it, *I* didn't have much choice in the matter. You told me that you loved him and that you didn't love me.'

'I was lying,' she whispered huskily. 'I did love you, very, very much, but...'

'You loved him more,' he offered cynically.

'Yes,' she agreed, tears filling her eyes, 'or at least I believed that I did. Please help me, Luke,' she implored him. 'I don't know who else to turn to.'

'Go and see this man—he's a first-class divorce lawyer,' he told her stiffly, scribbling a name and address down on a piece of paper and handing it to her without looking at her.

That had been six weeks ago. He had not seen or heard from her since, but he had not stopped thinking about her, remembering... She had been eighteen to his twenty-two; all Eve, all woman, teasing him, taunting him, laughing at him as he was unable to prevent himself from showing how he felt about her. It had been his first real experience of the intensity of emotional and physical love. And his last. He had been determined on that. Never again would any woman be allowed to put him through what she had—the pain, the self-contempt, the sheer intensity of emotions that had led only to the destruction of his pride and the humiliation of watching her walk away with another man. Any woman...no matter who she might be.

Oh yes, he had seen the look in Fenella's eyes as she sat opposite him and had guessed just what she was thinking. Her husband, despite his title and his wealth, or maybe because of them, was not the kind of man a woman would dream of having as her lover. A man's man was generally how others described him, if they wanted to be tactful and generous. Overweight, boorish, self-opinionated, a traditionalist who said openly that he believed a woman's place was in the home and, his be-

ing closer now to fifty than forty, it was understandable,
Luke acknowledged cynically, why Fenella might prefer
a generous divorce settlement and the chance to find
herself a more congenial and appealing man. But that
man was most definitely not going to be him.

Jenny was putting the final touches to the icing on the
twins' decorative birthday cake when Joss came bursting
in. Predictably, Louise had announced earlier in that
slightly bossy way that characterised her that they did
not want their cake decorated with sickly, yukky flowers
and things.

'What *do* you want, then?' Jenny had asked her,
slightly exasperated. Both the girls were due to start university at the beginning of the autumn term and whilst
she knew she was going to miss them, as she had commented ruefully to Jon, there were going to be certain
advantages to their departure. The lack of arguments
over their constant breaking of what Jenny considered
to be a perfectly reasonable and even overgenerous cur-
few during school term time was one thing, and the other
was the ability to go into her wardrobe without discovering that the very thing she wanted to wear was missing, presumed grubby and crumpled on the twins' bedroom floor.

'Something serious and meaningful,' Louise had responded in answer to her mother's wry question. She
had given her father a lofty look as he teased, 'Oh, you
mean something like the Benjamin Bunny cake you
drove us all crazy over...?'

'That was years ago,' she protested, turning her back
on him as she informed her mother, 'No. What we want
is something that shows what Katie and I are planning
to do with our lives.'

'Oh, you mean a replica of your mother's car with the

petrol tank empty and a scraped front number plate,' Jon offered helpfully.

'No, that is *not* what I mean,' Louise informed her father frostily, adding, 'and anyway it wasn't me who cracked the number plate, and as for the petrol... Do you *know* how much petrol actually costs?'

'I have a fair idea, yes,' Jon agreed mildly, causing Jenny to remind them both firmly that they were straying off the subject.

'Oh, you know, Mum...something with a bit of a legal flavour to it.'

In the end, having got no further help from either of her daughters, Jenny had opted for a huge, plain iced cake decorated in darker icing with the scales of Justice.

'Mum,' Joss demanded, throwing down his school bag before going straight to the fridge and opening the door.

'Joss, supper will be ready in half an hour,' Jenny reminded him firmly, adding, 'and you're late. Where have you been?'

'Mum, you know you said I could take a friend to the party on Saturday?' Joss reminded her, ignoring her question.

'I did say that, yes,' Jenny agreed cautiously, 'but...'

As a special treat Jon had announced that he had booked a large suite at the Grosvenor so that the girls and Jenny could get changed without worrying about crumpling their dresses on the journey from home and so that they did not have to travel back again until the morning after the party. Now Jenny, who had been planning to make sure that Joss went up to bed well before the party ended, wondered if they were going to be called upon to provide accommodation for Joss's friend, as well.

'You know we're all staying overnight at the Grosvenor, Joss?' she warned her son, 'and I don't know if your friend—'

'That's all right. I…I've arranged to meet them there,' Joss told her hurriedly.

'Oh well, in that case,' Jenny agreed, relieved. There were innumerable things she still had to do and typically Louise had suddenly started being difficult about the outfit she had decided to wear, claiming that she had never wanted a dress at all and that she would much rather have worn trousers.

'Mum, about my friend…' Joss began excitedly.

But Jenny shook her head and told him impatiently, 'Not now, Joss, please. I've got a hundred and one things left to do and you really ought to go and make a start on your homework before supper.'

'But, Mum,' Joss protested.

'Homework,' Jenny commanded firmly, adding, 'and while you're upstairs you might remind Jack that he still hasn't produced his sports kit and if he wants it clean for football practice tomorrow…'

'I'll tell him,' Joss agreed, going through the kitchen and heading for the stairs and the large, comfortably furnished bedroom-cum-study he shared with his cousin Jack, who had been living with them since the break-up of his parents' marriage and the disappearance of his father, David.

Jack's mother, Tania, after a long period of rehabilitation at a special centre for the treatment of people with eating disorders, was now living with her parents on the South Coast. Not yet entirely recovered from the years of suffering from bulimia, she had asked Jenny and Jon if Jack, her son, could continue to live with them.

Jenny had been happy to agree. In the time that he had been with them, Jack had become almost another son, the blood tie between him and her own children very close; their fathers were twins and everyone, but most importantly Jack himself, felt that it was better for him to remain in his present stable and familiar surroundings than to be uprooted to move south to live with his mother and maternal grandparents.

Although only two years separated them in age, at twelve going on thirteen to Joss's ten, Jack had already entered puberty whereas Joss had not. Both boys got on well together, but Jack was now virtually a teenager growing towards young manhood, whilst Joss in many ways was still a boy, and being male, neither of them was inclined to confide in the other. Since Jack was engrossed in reading a sports magazine when Joss walked into their shared bedroom, the younger boy saw no reason to tell him about his encounter with Bobbie or inform him of the fact that he had invited her to his sisters' party.

Possessed of a sunny, happy temperament with little inclination to brood or go looking for trouble and a logical way of reasoning things, it simply hadn't occurred to Joss that his parents might not view with equanimity the discovery that his 'friend' and their guest at the party was not another ten-year-old boy but, in fact, a twenty-six-year-old woman.

It *had* occurred to Bobbie, though, as she ruefully admitted during the course of her telephone call home, surreptitiously timed so that she could speak to her sister when no one else was about to overhear them.

'It's the perfect access to the family and right into the heart of it, Sam,' Bobbie admitted a little reluctantly. 'I couldn't believe it when he introduced himself to me as Joss Crighton.'

'And how old did you say this kid was?' Samantha Miller demanded of her sister.

'I'm not sure, somewhere around ten or maybe eleven. He's a real cutie, huge brown eyes and thick hair.'

'Sounds great,' Samantha commented enthusiastically.

Bobbie laughed. 'Oh, he is!'

'And you say he's asked you to his sisters' eighteenth birthday party?'

'Mmm…'

'What else did you find out? Did you—'

'No, not yet,' Bobbie interrupted her sister quickly. 'We were a bit public for me to cross-question him too deeply and we might have been overheard. I don't want anyone getting suspicious of either of us.'

'Cross-question, I like that,' Samantha told her grimly.

'How are things at home?' Bobbie asked, her voice suddenly becoming slightly tense and anxious. 'How is Mom?'

'She doesn't have a clue,' Samantha assured her, 'although even if I say so myself I am doing rather a good job of running interference for you. The first couple of days you were gone she was going crazy, asking me if I knew where you were, if there was some man… Poor Mom, she's just so desperate to get at least one of us married off.'

'What did you tell her?' Bobbie asked.

'I said you'd mentioned something about needing to get away now that you aren't seeing Nat any more.'

'Oh thanks. So now she'll be thinking I'm suffering from a broken heart,' Bobbie told her sister indignantly.

'Having her thinking that is better than having her guess the truth. When is this party by the way? We don't have a lot of time, not if…'

'No, I know. It's on Saturday, at the Grosvenor in Chester where, as good luck has it, I'm staying. It will be the perfect opportunity, not just for me to find out as much as I can from Joss, but also to study the family in general.'

'Do you think *you-know-who* will be there?' Samantha asked, her voice suddenly tensing and becoming brittle with hostility and anger.

'I don't know.'

'When I think of what they've done, the unhappiness they've caused...'

'I know, I know....' Bobbie paused, then said, 'Look, Sam, I'd better go. I'll ring you after the party and tell you what I've managed to find out.'

She was just about to replace the receiver when she remembered something she had omitted to tell her sister.

'I nearly forgot,' she hastened to add. 'You'll never guess what...' Laughing ruefully, she proceeded to tell Samanatha about Joss's descriptions of, and revelations about, his Chester cousins.

'What? Cousin Luke sounds like a real ape,' came Samantha's immediate and gutsy response, 'the type that goes for cutesy, brain-dead little blonde bimbos he can wear like a Band-Aid on his pathetic inadequacies. Personally, I've always preferred to judge a man by the size and warmth of his heart, not—'

'Sam...' Bobbie warned her sister, laughing.

'What? Oh! What a thing to suggest. I meant size as in height and not...' Samantha began in wounded dignity, only to break down in a fit of giggles. 'Well, good luck with Cousin Luke,' she teased her sister before ringing off. 'He sounds the perfect match for you, Bobbie, everything you've always wanted in a man.'

'Doesn't he just,' Bobbie agreed with heavy irony.

After she had replaced the receiver, she walked over to her window and stared unseeing through the glass. It was no mere whim or casual impulse that had brought her to England, to Chester, to Haslewich, but rather a quest that had been a part of both her and her twin sister's lives for as long as they had been old enough to understand the story of their mother's life.

Sombrely Bobbie walked back towards the bed. She supposed she would have to find something suitable to wear for this party. It had been difficult enough getting away without her mother asking what she was up to and without worrying about packing any kind of formal evening wear; as she knew, to her cost, when you were six foot plus, buying off the peg wasn't always an option.

In the small New England town where Bobbie and her sister had grown up, people were accustomed to their height; after all, it was a family trait. Dad was nearly six-five and his parents were tall, as well, and so were all their paternal kith and kin who were scattered around the area.

Stephen Miller's family could trace their ancestors right back to one of the founding Pilgrim families and it had not been easy for their mother to gain their acceptance in view of her own family background or rather… Fiercely Bobbie checked her thoughts. As Sam had told her before she left the States, it was high time that justice was done, the tables turned, and a certain person made to see just what they had lost through their pride and cruelty, and her own niggling sense of reluctance and unease had to be severely restrained.

CHAPTER TWO

'JENNY dear, I'm awfully sorry but I'm afraid I'm not going to be able to make it on Saturday after all.'

'Oh, Aunt Ruth,' Jenny protested into the telephone receiver. 'What's wrong?'

'Nothing's wrong,' Ruth assured her niece by marriage firmly. 'It's just that Olivia and Caspar's babysitter has let them down at the last minute and so I've offered to babysit Amelia for them instead. I don't think they've had a single night out since Amelia arrived eight months ago.'

'No, they haven't,' Jenny agreed. 'Jon tried to persuade Olivia not to rush back to work, but you know how conscientious she is, she insisted. At least during the summer holiday, Caspar has been at home to look after her.'

'Mmm... I know she's beginning to get a bit anxious because they haven't managed to find another suitable nanny as yet.'

'Poor girl, it must be so hard for her. I know how much she loves her work but I'd have hated to have to let someone else bring up my children especially when they were babies. When you read these stories of mothers giving up their babies, I often wonder... I know it's something that I could never bring myself to do. Ruth, are you still there?' she asked anxiously into the silent receiver.

'Yes, I'm still here,' Ruth answered crisply, adding, 'What you say is all very well, Jenny, but some women just don't have any option.'

'No, I realise that,' Jenny agreed sombrely, catching the faint note of criticism in Ruth's voice.

She had been lucky both in her marriage and more importantly in her husband, Jenny acknowledged as she replaced the receiver, very lucky.

'You're looking very pensive,' Jon commented as he came into the bedroom where Jenny had just been finishing packing their overnight cases when the phone rang. 'Not more problems?'

'Not exactly. Ruth just rang. She isn't going to be able to make it. She's offered to babysit for Olivia and Caspar. Apparently their original babysitter has let them down. I rather annoyed her, I think.'

'You?' Jon gave his wife an affectionate look as he took her in his arms. 'I doubt that, my love. You're far too kind-natured to annoy anyone.'

'Mmm… I did make rather a sweeping generalisation, I suppose,' she told him, explaining what had happened.

'Ah well, you know how hard Aunt Ruth has campaigned to raise funds for the town's special new mother and baby home.'

'Yes,' Jenny agreed. 'It's a very innovative idea. Ruth is determined that it won't be anything like the old unmarried mother and baby homes where girls used to be banished in disgrace if they were pregnant, and where the staff tried to persuade them to give their babies up for adoption.'

'To be fair, in those days it was generally believed that such children *were* better off being adopted,' Jon reminded her fair-mindedly.

'Mmm…I realise that. I suppose I just can't help thinking that if you hadn't married me when you did…'

'I know,' Jon told her gently, holding her tighter, 'and I know, as well, that you are as dedicated to raising money for this home as Ruth is. I ought to—you've persuaded me to part with enough money to help fund it.'

'Well, it *is* a good cause,' Jenny protested. 'We've bought the house and the land, and once it's been converted into small, private bedsitting rooms, we can give both the girls and their babies a protected environment.'

'Shall I take these cases down?' Jon asked, reminding her. 'You said you wanted to be at the Grosvenor early.'

'Yes, I know.' She glanced uncertainly at the telephone. 'I haven't rung Queensmead today, and—'

'Dad will be fine,' Jon assured her firmly. 'He's got Max and Madeleine with him, remember?'

'I know,' Jenny replied worriedly, 'but you know how impatient Max can be.'

'Yes, I do, but Madeleine will make sure that Dad's all right. You know how fond of him she is.'

'And him of her. It's ironic, really, isn't it, that the only woman he really approves of is one who isn't related to him by blood?'

'That's because Madeleine is the perfect stereotype of what Dad believes a woman should be,' Jon told her dryly.

'She's a lovely person,' Jenny countered. 'Kind, gentle, generous and...'

'Vulnerable?' Jon suggested.

They looked at one another in silence.

'I must admit I was surprised when we first met her after Max announced they were getting married.'

'Mmm...me, too. I wonder if he'd have been as keen to marry her if her father hadn't been who he is,' Jon speculated cynically.

'Oh, Jon, don't say that,' Jenny protested. 'She loves him so much.'

'Too much, perhaps?' Jon asked her.

'She seems so happy.'

'She's happy because Max is happy and Max is happy

because at the moment he's getting what he wanted. Whether or not he'll continue to be happy is another matter.'

Again they exchanged looks. Max might be their son but in temperament and outlook he was much closer and always had been to his uncle David than to either of them, although it hurt them both to admit it. Jenny knew that Max was a selfish and egotistical man who was ruthlessly determined in whatever he did.

Half past seven. Bobbie glanced up from her secluded position in the hotel lobby. She had tucked herself away in a shadowy corner so that she could see everyone who came into the hotel without being noticed herself—not an easy feat given her height and the colour and luxurious vibrancy of her hair.

She had already seen Joss arrive with another slightly older boy and a couple who must be his parents. Joss's hair was slicked back and the formality of his clothes made him look younger rather than older. She had hidden a smile.

Now the early arrivals for the party were beginning to gather in the lobby—a cheerful, happy crowd spanning the generations, who quite plainly all seemed to know one another from the greetings they were exchanging.

Joss's parents arrived back downstairs, his mother looking elegant in a dress that Bobbie's judicious and expert inspection informed her was very probably an Armani. Nice, very nice, she acknowledged as she watched the way the cream crêpe moved elegantly with Jenny's body.

The diamonds in her ears and around her neck were quite obviously real, and to judge both from the venue they had chosen for their twin daughters' birthday celebration and the appearance of their guests, financial hardship was not a problem that afflicted the Crighton family. But then, she had already known that, hadn't she? Already known all about their pride and arrogance, their belief that they were somehow better than anyone else and most certainly better than... She frowned as a fresh batch of guests arrived, her attention caught, oddly enough, not by the imposing height of the man walking so purposefully into the hotel, but rather the air, the aura of tautly controlled energy and impatience he seemed to bring with him.

'Luke,' she heard Joss's father exclaiming as he went forward to welcome him with a smile and a handshake, 'and James,' he added warmly as he turned to the man following behind him.

Luke and James. She had known who he was immediately, of course, Bobbie acknowledged, unaware of the dangerous allocation and use of the word 'he' in the singular rather than 'they' in the plural.

He was every bit as tall as Joss had told her, she admitted, and as for the rest...certainly he was an extremely physically powerful-looking and charismatically masculine-looking man, but she detected a certain hardness and hauteur...a coldness about him that in her view more than outweighed the appeal of his really too stunning good looks. There was, after all, such a thing as overkill, and rather like a strong perfume the effect of his physical magnetism was too overpowering to be attractive, a turn-off rather than a turn-on, she decided disparagingly.

The tiny, fragile-looking little blonde clinging to his arm obviously didn't share her view, though. She was gazing up at him adoringly and extremely possessively, Bobbie noticed as Luke turned to introduce her to Joss's parents, and on closer inspection she was not quite so young as her girlishly feminine silk dress seemed to proclaim. In her thirties rather than her twenties, Bobbie

guessed, and very adept at using her delicacy to create
the impression of being somewhat younger. He would,
of course, go for that type. Bobbie's contempt for him
grew.

Luke was having a hard time keeping the impatience
out of his voice as he introduced Fenella to Jon and
Jenny. He was still infuriated at the way she'd managed
to inveigle herself into being included in their party,
tricking James into agreeing to pick her up by giving
him the impression, deliberately so, Luke knew, that he
had invited her as his partner, when in fact...

'What is she doing here?' he had demanded half an
hour earlier when, as arranged, James had called round
to collect him and he had seen Fenella sitting demurely
in the back of James's car.

'She rang me up and asked me to collect her,' James
had informed him, looking both upset and uncomfortable
when Luke had told him pithily that he had been deceived and that there was no way he had ever intended
asking Fenella.

'Oh, but she said—' he began, but Luke cut him short.

'I don't give a damn *what* she said, James,' he
snapped testily. '*I* am telling you that she tricked you
and that I most certainly did not invite her to come with
us. God knows how she even knew about tonight in the
first place.'

'Oh, I think that's probably my fault,' James confessed. 'I bumped into her in town while you were in
Brussels and we got talking and I mentioned the party.
She said she knew all about it and that you were taking
her and...' James looked uncomfortable. 'I know that
you and she...and I thought...well...'

'You *know* that she and I *what*?' Luke demanded
grimly, answering his own question by continuing, 'We
dated for a while a long time ago, yes, a *long* time ago,'
he underlined. 'She approached me for advice about her

divorce and that is the only kind of contact I have had with her since her marriage, and that's the only kind of contact I *intend* to have with her. She's poison, James,' Luke warned his younger brother. 'Take my word for it.'

Poison she indeed was, and infuriated though he might be by the way she was clinging to him like a piece of ivy, good manners and a very male disinclination to cause a scene prevented Luke from disengaging her arm from his and walking off and disowning her.

'Fenella...what's it,' Jon commented quietly to Jenny after they had disappeared to remove their coats. 'Isn't she the one that Luke used to...?'

'Mmm...I think so,' Jenny agreed.

'I thought she was married to Sir Peter Longton,' Jon remarked.

'She is,' Jenny confirmed. 'Or rather she was. Apparently they're going to divorce.'

'Well...I doubt that will please Luke!'

Jenny shot her husband a questioning look. 'Won't it? They are here together.'

'They are certainly both here but, reading Luke's body language, they are not, definitely not, together,' Jon informed her. 'And if she is hoping that Luke will prove as malleable as a man as he was as a boy, I suspect she's going to be doomed to disappointment.'

As Jon and Jenny gently swept their guests towards the private suite they had reserved for the party, Joss started to search the foyer anxiously. It was eight o'clock.

'Joss,' Jenny called out as she saw her youngest child hovering by the entrance.

'I won't be a moment,' Joss told her, excitement giving way to disappointment and anxiety as he searched the foyer a second time for his new friend.

Jenny frowned. She had almost forgotten that Joss had told her that he wanted to invite a friend.

'Come on, Mum,' Louise demanded.

Jenny gave Joss an uncertain look. He was, after all, only ten years old, but the lobby of the Grosvenor was surely a safe enough place for him to be allowed to wait for his friend on his own for a few minutes whilst she checked that everything was in order in their private suite.

Bobbie waited until Jon and Jenny had disappeared before standing up and quietly making her way across to where Joss stood anxiously staring towards the main hotel doors. She touched him lightly on the arm, causing him to jump and then turn round, his anxious expression giving way to one of beaming delight as he saw her.

'You're here. I thought you must have changed your mind.'

'No, I haven't changed my mind,' Bobbie assured him.

He was so kind and open, so…so young and vulnerable; the lessons life taught him now would be indelibly etched on his personality. Did she really want it on her conscience that she…?

'Come on,' Joss was urging her. 'It's this way.'

It was not her job to take on the responsibility for Joss's emotions, she reminded herself sternly as she turned to follow him. She was here for a different purpose, a very different purpose, which reminded her…

As Joss pushed open the double doors and stood back for her to precede him into the large, well-packed room, she turned to him and commented, 'My, that sure is a lot of people. I guess all your family must be here.'

'Almost,' Joss agreed, his eyes clouding a little as he informed her, 'Great-Aunt Ruth isn't here, though.'

'Great-Aunt Ruth,' Bobbie marvelled after a second's pause during which she kept her eyes firmly on the elegantly decorated room with its artistic and impressive swags and garlands of natural greenery and flowers. She had a small gift in that direction herself and because of it was well aware of the time and skill that must have gone into first conceiving the idea for the decorations and then putting it into practical use in order to achieve such an apparently artless and 'natural' effect. 'She sounds very formidable. I guess she's not a party person....'

'She *was* going to come,' Joss informed her, 'but she's babysitting for Olivia and Caspar instead. That's them over there,' he told Bobbie helpfully, indicating a couple who stood talking to Joss's parents.

The woman was about her own age, Bobbie guessed, in her mid- to late twenties, the man with her a little older. She was stylishly dressed, her hair cut in an immaculate shiny bob, and Bobbie studied her carefully before turning back to Joss.

'I do wish Aunt Ruth were here,' Joss was telling her. 'I wanted you to meet her.'

Once again Bobbie found it easier to study her surroundings rather than meet Joss's eyes. 'Well, I'd like to meet her, too,' she returned lightly. 'I guess we'll have to try to fix something up before I move on.

'Oh my,' she exclaimed, her attention suddenly caught by the man leaning casually against the wall on the opposite side of the room. Handsome simply wasn't the word to describe him, she acknowledged; if a man could be described as 'beautiful' without in any way detracting from the sheer male animal magnetism of him, then this man was.

From the top of his shiny, well-groomed dark hair to the tip of his evening shoes, he epitomised everything that was masculine and good-looking. He would have made a perfect movie star, Bobbie thought, a heartthrob in the true, old-fashioned sense of the word.

'Who is that?'

'That's Max,' Joss told her in an oddly flat voice, adding reluctantly, 'He's my brother.'

His *brother*. Now Bobbie *was* surprised and, as she turned from watching Joss's face close up and his eyes become slightly shadowed to study the handsome six-footer leaning so slouchily against the wall, she asked him ruefully, 'So why wasn't *he* mentioned when you were cataloguing your family's available males?'

'Because he isn't…available, that is,' Joss answered in that same flat voice. 'Max is married.'

'Oh, I see.' Vainly Bobbie searched the room looking for the woman who would be the kind of mate such a man would undoubtedly choose—the female equivalent of himself. Stunning, almost theatrically good-looking and possessed of that same head-turning charismatic appeal he patently had in such abundance.

'That's Madeleine, his wife, over there,' Joss told her, obviously guessing what she was doing and then adding quickly and almost defensively as Bobbie studied the woman he had indicated, 'She's nice. I like her.'

'I'm sure she is,' Bobbie agreed gravely as she took in Madeleine's plain face and slightly dumpy figure, acknowledging two things. One, that Max must either be completely and utterly head over heels in love with her, or two, he must have some other equally powerful and compelling reason for marrying her. Bobbie suspected she knew which.

'Why don't we hire someone to make enquiries for us before we do anything?' Bobbie had suggested when they had first discussed the matter, a little queasily aware of how uncomfortable she would feel prying into other people's private business, but Samantha had shaken her head forcefully.

'We can't…take the risk of involving anyone else,'

she reminded her sister. 'We're going to have to do it ourselves.'

'You mean *I'm* going to have to do it,' Bobbie retorted feelingly. 'After all, you can't just take off for Europe. Not now you're halfway through your master's.'

'No, I can't,' Samantha agreed cheerfully, then added teasingly, 'You should have come with me when I took that couple of years out and travelled. We have to go through with this, Bobbie,' she went on to say more seriously. 'Remember all those years ago how we said we would?'

'Yes, I remember,' Bobbie had agreed. How could she have forgotten the childhood vow she and Sam had made? 'I just hate the feeling that we're doing anything underhand...spying...'

'*Us* do anything underhand?' Sam had shouted bitterly.

Silently Bobbie looked down now at Joss.

'Where are your sisters?' she asked him conversationally.

'Over there,' he replied, indicating the pair of identical twins who stood chatting with what was obviously a large group of shared friends. They were, Bobbie was pleased to note, wearing completely different outfits and had completely different hairstyles, but there was still no mistaking those shared inherited features.

'My goodness, who on earth is that with Joss?' Jenny exclaimed, having caught sight of her youngest child for the first time since he had entered the room.

'She's certainly not someone you could fail to notice, is she?' Olivia laughed as she, too, studied the endearingly odd combination of a very youthful Joss and the magnificently eye-catching young woman who was with him.

'She reminds me of a lioness,' Jenny murmured, 'all golden grace and power. I wonder where Joss met her?'

'I think I know,' Jon informed them, having turned round to see what was occupying his wife's attention. 'Minnie Cooke at the wine bar mentioned that Joss had been in the other day with a tall blonde American.'

'American, eh... I think I'd just better go over and say hello...a fellow countrywoman and all that.'

'Caspar,' Olivia warned, adding firmly, 'We'll *both* go over.'

As families went, this one certainly liked to give the impression that it was protective of its own, Bobbie reflected cynically as she registered the interest she was beginning to excite amongst certain adult members of Joss's family.

Max had already prised his shoulders off their resting place on the wall to give her a lazy once-over. Luke, peering past the head of his blonde companion, had sent a look of frowning scrutiny in her direction. Jenny appeared frankly astonished and now here was Olivia with Caspar in tow bearing down on them.

Bobbie held her breath and then counted to ten before easing herself into her chosen role.

'Hello there.' Olivia smiled warmly, extending her hand towards Bobbie. 'You must be Joss's friend.'

'I hope so,' Bobbie responded with equal warmth, shaking Olivia's hand firmly as she introduced herself. 'Bobbie Miller. Bobbie being short for Roberta.'

'I'm Olivia Johnson, Joss's cousin, and this is Caspar, my husband.'

By the time Caspar had returned with the drinks that Olivia had dispatched him to fetch for them, she had elicited the information that Bobbie, having finished her studies, was taking time out to 'do' Europe before returning home to work in her father's law firm.

'So your father's a lawyer...what a coincidence. Our family, the Crightons, are nearly all involved in the law in one form or another.'

'Dad *was* an attorney,' Bobbie informed her carefully. 'Right now he's in Congress.'

'So what exactly brought you to Haslewich?' Caspar asked cheerfully, handing Bobbie her drink. 'It's not exactly on the normal tourist route.'

'No,' Bobbie agreed. 'I guess I just got kinda interested in the place when I overheard someone talking about it in Chester, so I thought I'd drive out and take a look around. That's when I met Joss.'

'She was in the churchyard,' Joss informed them.

'It feels rather scary to see those headstones with dates going back so far,' Bobbie cut in... 'I guess your family must have been in the town for centuries.'

'Not really,' Olivia responded. 'The Crightons came originally from Chester, but our branch of it broke away at the beginning of this century. So far as putting down our roots in Haslewich goes, we're relative newcomers.' Then conversationally she asked, 'Are you planning to stay in the area long?'

'I wasn't going to, but I'd booked myself into the Grosvenor as a small treat before I realised how expensive it was and I guess I'm going to have to look around for some kind of temporary work so that I can earn a little money before I move on.'

Olivia listened speculatively as she saw Bobbie's rueful expression and then frowned as she glanced at her watch and told Caspar, 'I'd better go and ring Aunt Ruth and check that everything's okay. Our nanny left us unexpectedly—her mother isn't very well and since I'm now back at work in the family law practice and Caspar goes back to university next week, we're desperately trying to find a replacement. I don't suppose you know anything about child care...?' Olivia half joked.

Bobbie took a deep breath. 'Well now, it just so happens that I do,' she returned lightly. 'I spent the last year of high school and nearly all of my college vacations helping out at a…at a special local crèche…'

'Really.' Olivia gave her a searching glance and asked her, 'If you were serious about looking for a job, perhaps we could get together and have a chat?'

'Sure,' Bobbie agreed warmly.

'I'll be in touch,' Olivia promised her as she hurried off to make her telephone call.

'Wow, that would be great if you did stay on,' Joss enthused.

'Well, that's up to Olivia to decide,' Bobbie warned him. 'I'm not a qualified nanny and—'

'But I could tell that she really liked you and so did Caspar,' Joss interrupted her enthusiastically.

'Well, I kinda liked them, as well,' Bobbie agreed—and meant it—but her conscience was beginning to trouble her a little.

Back home, the plans she and Sam had made had seemed perfectly logical, but now… She had liked Olivia and Caspar, and as for Joss… She frowned as she looked down and saw that he was scowling. A quick glance across the room told her why; Max was walking purposefully towards them.

'Well now, young Joss, and who exactly is this?'

Bobbie sympathised with Joss as she watched the tip of his ears burning a furious red at his brother's deliberately condescending manner towards him.

'Hi, I'm Bobbie,' Bobbie introduced herself calmly.

The dark eyebrows lifted. 'An American… Oh dear, Joss, you will be popular with the old man. Our grandfather, I'm afraid to say, has an aversion to Americans,' he told Bobbie.

Joss, Bobbie could see, was looking miserably embarrassed.

'That's okay,' she responded easily. 'My grandfather feels exactly the same way about you British.'

Max gave her a narrow-eyed look. 'Hopefully not an aberration you've inherited,' he suggested softly.

'Who says it's an aberration?' Bobbie replied and had the satisfaction of seeing the extraordinary effect of his amazing physical good looks dimmed by the unpleasant expression in his eyes.

No wonder Joss was so wary around him.

'Oh, Max, there you are. I—'

'Oh, for God's sake, Maddie, must you follow me around like an idiotic sheepdog?' Max demanded irritably as he turned towards his wife.

Bobbie felt for her as the other woman's face burned a painful dark red. Joss was chewing the side of his cheek and Bobbie herself had to suppress an urge to tell Max exactly what she thought of his arrogance and cruelty.

'Your husband and I were just discussing our respective grandfathers,' Bobbie informed Madeleine with a genuinely friendly smile.

'Oh, I see.' She had a shy, hesitant voice and a very uncertain manner, Bobbie noticed as Madeleine went on to tell her, 'It's a shame that Ben can't be here tonight. He had a fall some years ago and it's left him with a very painful and rheumaticky hip joint that the doctors say he should have replaced.'

Relief wiped the tense anxiety from Madeleine's face. Poor soul, she obviously lived in fear and dread of losing her husband. She need not, Bobbie decided. Like the fancy icing on an otherwise repulsively unappealing cake, those good looks were all that there was to him.

She didn't want to totally alienate Max, though, she acknowledged. He could prove to be a valuable source of information.

So his grandfather had an aversion to Americans, did he? He wasn't the only member of the Crighton family who felt like that as she had good cause to know.

CHAPTER THREE

Two hours later, Bobbie broke off in mid-banter with Saul to whom she had been comfortably chatting very happily for the past twenty minutes or so, recognising guiltily that not only was it over half an hour since she had last seen Joss, but that she was also actually enjoying herself.

It had been Olivia who had introduced her to Saul and Saul himself who had explained ruefully to her that he was currently in Louise's bad books. 'She wanted me to partner her this evening, but as I told her, as a divorced man in my mid-thirties and her cousin to boot, I'm hardly the right partner for her.'

'Which naturally makes you all the more attractive to her,' Bobbie had agreed mock-gravely. 'Come on, admit it,' she had coaxed him humorously. 'It must be quite some ego boost to have as stunningly pretty an eighteen-year-old as Louise crazily in love with you.'

'Just occasionally, yes, it is,' Saul had agreed openly, 'but the rest of the time quite frankly it's rather terrifying, which just goes to show how old I actually am getting.'

'I really ought to go and find Joss,' Bobbie now told Saul.

It was so frustrating having the opportunity to meet and mix with the family at such close hand and yet at the same time feeling restrained from asking what she really wanted to know just in case they should guess what she was up to.

'The last time I saw him he was talking with Luke.' He paused when he saw Bobbie's expression. 'You don't like Luke? You're in a minority,' he assured her. 'Most of your sex appear to find him extremely attractive.'

'But I am not most women,' Bobbie informed him firmly.

'No, you aren't, are you?' Saul agreed softly.

Smiling at him, Bobbie shook her head and turned away. She had spotted Joss on the other side of the room, and as Saul had said, he was talking to Luke. Bobbie started to make her way towards them.

The evening had done nothing to improve Luke's mood. Fenella had proved to be every bit as clingy and possessive as he had feared, subtly managing to create the impression amongst his family that they were something of an 'item' and making it impossible for him to refute her allusions without causing a public scene.

He had no intention of letting her get away with it, though. Before they parted company tonight, she was going to be left in no doubt whatsoever that the past was quite definitely over and there was no place for her in his present or his future, in any shape or form.

''Oh, I'm staying at the Grosvenor,' he heard her saying softly now to one of his aunts, giving him an adoring sideways look as she confided, 'Luke thought it best in the circumstances. After all, officially I'm still married.' She paused delicately whilst Luke watched his aunt's head nodding sagely.

Ignoring Fenella, he turned towards Joss and joked, 'So where did you find the quarterback, Joss?'

Bobbie, who was just within earshot, ground her teeth in silent outrage. She was used to comments about her height, of course, but there was nothing remotely unfeminine or gross about her—quite the opposite.

As he saw the look on Joss's face, Luke cursed himself under his breath. It wasn't fair of him to vent his irritation and fire at Fenella's manipulative behaviour on Joss, even if there was something about the stately, almost queenly stunning beauty of the unknown woman he had brought into their midst that brought the tiny hairs on the back of his neck to prickle with atavistic awareness. Perhaps it was something about that thick, honey-coloured mass of glorious hair, or perhaps it was the way she carried her impressive height and her even more impressive body. Perhaps it was just something about her manner, or perhaps the reason lay much closer to home, within his own emotional consciousness that he couldn't somehow dismiss.

She might not be the type to actively go looking for a fight, but she certainly wasn't going to run from this particular one, Bobbie decided as she ignored the temptation in the face of Luke's taunting overheard comment to pretend she hadn't heard and simply walk away. Instead she stalked purposefully to where he and Joss were standing, bestowing on Joss the beneficence of a multiwatt smile whilst cleverly managing to angle her body so that she could also look Luke Crighton straight in the eye... well, almost straight in the eye. Joss had not lied about his height and it was oddly disconcerting to be forced to tilt her chin upwards to meet his dispassionate gaze.

'You must be Luke,' Bobbie announced, taking the initiative before Joss could introduce them.

'Must I?' Luke asked her dryly. 'Now why, I wonder, should you assume that?'

'Oh, it wasn't an assumption,' Bobbie told him breezily. 'I recognised you from Joss's description...or rather his description of your addiction to a certain type of female accessory. I shouldn't worry too much about it,' she told him with a kind voice. 'They do say it's a phase that most men grow out of once they mature.'

Out of the corner of her eye, Bobbie could see Joss looking worriedly from Luke to herself. It wasn't really fair of her to involve him, she acknowledged.

'Come on, Joss,' she invited him mischievously. 'It looks like they're serving the buffet and a girl my size needs one heck of a lot of feeding.'

Joss looked relieved as he heard the note of humour in her voice, but one glance at Luke's stern face warned Bobbie that he wasn't deceived and that he certainly wasn't about to overlook or ignore her comment about his girlfriend.

'Well, I guess we can scratch Luke off our list,' Bobbie told Joss ruefully as they headed for the buffet.

'Fenella isn't really his girlfriend,' Joss informed her eagerly. 'I heard James telling Dad that Luke was angry with him for letting Fenella trick him into bringing her. She and Luke used to go out with one another a long time ago, but she's married to someone else now, although James says that she's going to divorce him.'

Which would explain why Luke was so anxious to distance himself publicly from any kind of intimate relationship with her, at least until such time as the divorce was final, Bobbie realised. A man in his position would not want to have any hint, any breath of scandal affecting his reputation.

It had been immediately obvious to her that Luke had that particular brand of prideful male arrogance that she had always found aggravating and unappealing. Dominant Alpha-type men had never held any kind of attraction for her. She preferred men like those she had grown up closest to, gentle men whose strength lay in their ability to be kind and compassionate—to have emotions.

Katie and Louise had opted for an informal arrangement of round tables for eight for the buffet meal without any set table plan, and Joss and Bobbie had just settled themselves down at one of these, their plates satisfyingly heaped with a generous selection from the mouth-watering dishes being served, when they were joined by Olivia and Caspar.

Bobbie, who had been watching with amusement a small piece of byplay between Saul and Louise and mentally concluding that Saul was deceiving himself if he thought that Louise was going to give up on her determined pursuit of him, smiled warmly at them as they sat down.

Unlike Luke, these were two of Joss's relatives she actively liked.

'I hope you don't mind our joining you,' Olivia commented, 'but hearing your voice has made Caspar feel positively homesick.'

'No such thing,' Caspar objected. 'Not that it isn't good to hear a familiar American accent,' he added, turning to Bobbie.

'He's a typical Philadelphia lawyer,' Olivia told Bobbie, pulling a wry face.

Caspar shook his head and informed them both that he was now a university lecturer and not a lawyer.

'Technically maybe, but you did qualify in law and that's the subject you lecture in,' Olivia reminded him. 'Honestly, you'd think that having come from a family that's more or less obsessed by the law I'd have rebelled and picked a husband who did something else,' Olivia mock complained to Bobbie, whilst Caspar laughed and tugged gently on her silky bob, teasing her. 'Well, sharing a common career gives us something to talk about, and unlike other married couples, we're never going to be able to complain that we find each other's careers uninteresting.'

'I would guess from your accent that you're from New England,' Caspar commented to Bobbie.

'You guess right,' Bobbie confirmed with a smile. 'I was born and raised in a small town some ways north of Boston, but since my dad became involved in politics my folks spend a good part of their time in Washington.'

'Do you come from a large family?' Olivia asked her.

'Some,' Bobbie replied cautiously, 'On Dad's side...'

'Do you mind if we join you?'

Bobbie tensed as she looked up and saw Luke and Fenella standing on the opposite side of the table.

'No, of course not,' Olivia answered when the small pause that followed Luke's request had stretched just that little bit too far.

Deliberately avoiding any kind of eye contact with him, Bobbie turned to tell Joss approvingly how much she was enjoying the buffet.

'This salmon is delicious,' she told Olivia, forking up a second mouthful.

'Salmon...' Fenella gave a fastidious shrug. 'It's terribly fatty. I only ever eat white fish and of course I always have it steamed. Some people just have absolutely no idea about the amount of calories they can add to their food by not cooking it the right way. You've put on weight recently, Olivia. You must be what...a good size twelve now?' Fenella commented, eyeing Olivia assessingly.

'Must I...? I have to confess I really don't know,' Olivia returned easily. 'Since Amelia's birth the last thing on my mind has been my weight although, if anything, before I became pregnant, I do feel I was a little underweight. However, if I'm honest, I have to admit that I've been taking full advantage of the fact that breast-feeding allows you to eat generously.'

'Breast-feeding...?' Fenella's voice squeaked, her eyes almost popping. 'Oh, but surely...' Her eyes dropped betrayingly to the soft, womanly curves of Olivia's body before she bit her lip and looked away again. 'When I had Crispin I was adamant that I couldn't possibly feed him myself. I'm afraid I'm just not the earth-mother type.' She gave a small tinkly laugh, the expression in her eyes making Bobbie feel compassionately sorry for the unknown Crispin.

The easy atmosphere of friendly warmth had vanished from the table with the arrival of Luke and Fenella to be replaced by one that was guarded and slightly strained, and as she looked around the table, Bobbie knew that she wasn't alone in feeling this. Caspar's mouth had thinned as he listened to Fenella's comments. Olivia looked as though she wanted to respond more forcefully than she had but was trying to restrain herself.

'Oh, Luke, you know I said I didn't want any wine,' Fenella protested, nonetheless taking a delicate sip from the glass she had picked up and giving Luke a flirtatious glance from beneath her lashes as she demanded coyly, 'You wouldn't be trying to get me tipsy, would you?' then giving him a meaningful look.

Bobbie nearly choked on her food as she heard Caspar muttering exasperatedly under his breath, 'Not if he's got any sense,' and then had to fight to restrain her mirth as she saw the acid look Luke was giving her.

'It's a pity Aunt Ruth isn't here,' Joss mourned, oblivious to the adult melodrama going on around him. 'Salmon is *her* favourite, as well,' he informed Bobbie.

Bobbie put down her fork, the food on it untouched.

'Yes, you must meet Ruth before you leave the area,' Olivia broke in warmly. 'If you're really interested in learning more about the family, then Ruth is the best person for you to talk to.'

Luke was frowning as he looked at her, Bobbie realised.

'Is there any particular reason *why* you're interested in our family?' he asked Bobbie.

'No particular reason,' Bobbie countered calmly, unable to resist challenging him, 'Is there any particular reason why I shouldn't be?'

Fenella, obviously unwilling to share Luke's attention with anyone, gave Bobbie a baleful look as she leaned across the table between them, putting her hand possessively on Luke's arm and demanding, 'Let's dance, Luke. We used to dance so well together,' she told him huskily.

'Did we?' Luke grimaced. 'I must confess I don't remember.'

'Er…we really ought to go and talk to Saul and his parents, darling,' Olivia intervened quickly, pushing back her chair as she spoke.

'Yes. I shall have to be leaving soon,' Bobbie told Joss. 'But before I go, I must thank your parents.'

She, too, stood up, unwilling to witness the scene she could sense was about to follow as they all left Luke and Fenella at the table. Out of the corner of her eye, Bobbie could see Fenella pouting sulkily.

'Phew, poor old Luke,' Olivia commented once they were all out of earshot.

'He obviously must have found her attractive once,' Bobbie couldn't resist pointing out coolly.

'Well, yes,' Olivia agreed, 'but he was very, very young, only twenty-two, and I think he was disillusioned pretty quickly. You don't seem to like Luke very much,' Olivia stated with a lawyer's directness.

'Not much,' Bobbie agreed cheerfully.

'I'm sorry that Luke called you a quarterback,' Joss told Bobbie softly five minutes later when Bobbie had said her goodbyes to Olivia and Caspar.

'Well, I guess it's a kind of compliment,' Bobbie responded wryly. 'I reckon a major league quarterback gets paid a heck of a lot more than I'm ever likely to earn.

'Look, I can see your folks over there.' She directed Joss's attention to the gap in the dancers crowding the floor through which she could see his parents.

'I wish you didn't have to go,' Joss mourned as she made her way determinedly towards Jenny and Jon. 'But you're still going to be here for a while yet, aren't you?' he asked her, brightening.

'For a while,' Bobbie agreed cautiously.

There were things she had to do, information she needed to gain, which would be better accomplished out of sight of Joss's shrewd young eyes.

'Thank you for allowing me to gatecrash your party,' Bobbie said after reaching Joss's parents.

'You didn't gatecrash it,' Joss objected indignantly. 'I invited you.'

Jenny laughed. 'You're more than welcome,' she assured Bobbie warmly. 'I just hope that Joss hasn't taken up too much of your time or made a nuisance of himself,' she said, ruffling Joss's hair and smiling lovingly at him as she gave him a brief hug.

'No way,' Bobbie replied. 'I've enjoyed talking with him and hearing all about the Crighton family.'

It had been a long night, Bobbie acknowledged tiredly as she reached the sanctuary of her hotel bedroom and locked the door. She made her way to the bathroom, then stripped off her clothes whilst she ran a bath.

Half an hour later, she decided regretfully that she had soaked in the deliciously deep and steamy depths of the huge Edwardian-style tub for long enough, and besides, there was one last thing she had to do before she could finally go to bed. She dialled the number and then waited until she heard the familiar voice so very like her own.

'Can we talk? I couldn't wait until Sunday to talk to you,' she asked conspiratorially.

'Just,' came back the answer. 'They've just gone out. Okay, give. What have you found out?'

'Nothing much, other than the fact that certain members of the Crighton family are unbelievable, obnoxious and arrogant.'

'You had to travel all the way to England to discover

that?' Samantha questioned cynically. 'I thought we already—'

'Yes, I know. I'm sorry,' Bobbie apologised. 'It's just that…I'm not sure that what we're planning is a good idea, Sam. Tonight, talking with Olivia and Caspar, I—'

'Olivia and Caspar—who the heck are they?'

'Joss's cousin and her husband. He's an American from Philly, and—'

'Hey, have you any idea how much this call is costing? I knew I should have gone over there myself. The trouble with you is that you're just so darned soft-hearted and sentimental you'd find excuses for the devil himself. Bobbie, you know what the doctor…what happened last year…we may not have much time left and—'

'Dr Fraser said that she was fully one hundred percent recovered,' Bobbie protested, but underneath her fierce protestation she knew that her voice was betraying her anxiety and fear.

'Yes, I know,' Samantha agreed. 'But…we've got to see this through, Bobbie. We've got to do it. I just wish that I could be over there.…'

'You can't, not if you're going to get your master's and you *are* going to get it.'

'I know…I know. So come on, what have you managed to find out?'

'Nothing much. According to Joss and Olivia, Aunt Ruth is the person to talk to about the family's history.'

'Aunt Ruth?' There was a long pause and then Samantha's voice grew slightly fainter and huskier. 'Aunt Ruth, eh. Well now… So *are* you going to talk to her?'

'I don't know, Sam.' Bobbie's voice took on a troubled tone. 'To be honest, I just don't think that she'd be the right person.'

There was a long pause before she heard Samantha saying, 'Well, I guess you're probably right.'

After she had finished her telephone call, Bobbie poured herself a glass of Perrier water from the minibar and padded barefoot across to the window. The hotel bathrobe unexpectedly was just a little too long for her and certainly far too wide and had, she suspected, been found from somewhere by the eagle-eyed maid, who must have noticed how much taller she was than their average female guest. Full marks to her for her observation. There was something very comforting about wearing something so obviously too big; it made her feel positively fragile and dainty, Bobbie reflected ruefully, frowning as she heard someone knocking on her door.

She went to open it, her mouth rounding into a startled 'Oh' of surprise as she saw Luke Crighton standing in the corridor, holding her wrap.

'You left this downstairs,' he informed her.

'Yes…I did,' Bobbie agreed distantly, giving him a frosty look as she added, 'But there was no need for you to go to the trouble of returning it to me. I could have collected it in the morning.'

'I'm sure, but Jenny was anxious to get it back to you,' he told her smoothly.

He was standing well away from the door, too far away for her to reach out and take the wrap from him, forcing her to step out of the room and into the thankfully deserted corridor. She held out her hand for the wrap as she did so, having carefully made sure the door was on the latch beforehand. The last thing she wanted right now was to be locked out of her room wearing only a towelling robe, especially with someone like Luke Crighton to witness her potential embarrassment.

'My wrap,' she demanded crisply as she stepped towards him, but instead of handing it to her, to her astounded disbelief, Luke stepped up to her, catching her completely off guard as he skilfully caught up both her hands behind her back with one of his whilst using his free arm to force her into a parody of a lover's intimate embrace.

Instinctively Bobbie tried to free herself, twisting her body against the dual constraint of his hard-packed muscular body and the tight grip of his hand on her wrists and at the same time trying to lever her leg free to bring her knee up against the most vulnerable part of his body.

It didn't work; he let her work her leg free all right, but only so that he could take advantage of her accommodating movement by imprisoning her leg between both of his as he pushed her back against the wall of the corridor and bent his head purposefully towards her.

'Don't you dare… Oh, don't you dare,' Bobbie gasped indignantly, her own eyes blinking with fury as she saw the amused glint in his.

'No?' he mocked her, whispering the word against her mouth. 'What are you going to do to stop me?'

'This,' she grated fiercely, baring her teeth as she prepared to take a sharp bite at the male mouth hovering so predatorily close to her own, but instead of the look of cold distaste she had expected to see in Luke's eyes, he actually appeared to be laughing.

Bobbie glowered at him in indignation, but the furious tirade she had been about to deliver became a muffled choke of shocked astonishment as she saw him lift his hand, the one resting on the wall alongside her, towards her face and then slowly stroke her half-parted lips with the hard pad of his thumb before sliding one finger between her teeth until the tip of it made contact with her tongue.

His flesh tasted slightly salty—and wholly male. She shivered once in mute shock and then again in…in what? she tried to ask herself in the confusion that flooded her brain and her senses.

'Suck it,' she heard Luke whispering softly to her. 'It's sexy....'

'Luke...'

Bobbie thought she recognised that high-pitched feminine whine, but as she tried to turn her head to look down the corridor, Luke stopped her, blocking out her view as he covered her mouth with his.

'Luke.'

The voice was closer now and sharper. It was definitely Fenella's. Bobbie tried again to jerk her body away from Luke's.

He certainly knew how to kiss, she acknowledged dizzily. She hadn't been so instantly and gloriously affected by a mere kiss since she had dated her first crush in high school...and maybe not even then, she admitted to herself.

'Luke, how could you do this to me?' Fenella was screeching at what felt like only inches away from Bobbie's left ear. 'You know how much I love you....'

'I know nothing of the sort,' Luke returned dauntingly, having finally lifted his mouth from Bobbie's and turned his attention from her towards Fenella.

He still hadn't released her, though, Bobbie realised, and if she was honest with herself, she wasn't sure it would be a good idea to force herself away from him right now; her legs had become disconcertingly unsteady. And as for that look she had seen in Luke's eyes when he had finally lifted his mouth from hers... Bobbie felt her stomach start to quiver.

'You can't possibly prefer her to me,' Fenella protested in outrage.

'I not only can...I do,' Luke returned. Then ignoring Fenella, he turned back to Bobbie and said quite audibly in an amused voice, 'I know you have this fantasy about making love somewhere public, but I do think we would be rather more comfortable in your room...in private....'

And before Bobbie could stop him, he had pushed open her door and whisked them both inside. He proceeded to close it firmly behind him and then lock it almost before Bobbie could find time to draw breath.

When she did she was so angry that she could hardly find the words. 'What on earth do you think you're doing?' she demanded as she pulled herself free from his arms and faced him, praying that he would put the visible trembling of her body down to her anger and not the after-affects of his kiss.

'Isn't it obvious?' he asked her with clinical detachment.

'You used me to help you get rid of Fenella,' Bobbie accused. She shook her head and then pushed the heavy weight of her hair off her face. 'Why not simply tell her you didn't want her if you don't…? My God, what kind of man are you to deliberately come up here and use me, manipulate me, *plan*—'

'I didn't deliberately plan anything,' Luke interrupted her suavely. 'I simply seized the moment and took advantage of the opportunity the circumstances offered me when I saw Fenella coming down the corridor towards us.'

'You decided to make a grab for me and make out like the two of us were involved in some kind of passionate clinch…that we were… The moment wasn't the only thing you seized,' she berated him furiously, 'and if you think—'

'Calm down,' he advised her.

'Calm down! You grab hold of me, manhandle me…force me into my room and then you—'

'You're perfectly safe,' he interrupted in an unruffled voice, adding almost disparagingly, 'For a start, you're not my type.'

Not his type! Bobbie's eyes flashed warning signs of an impending major storm.

'I'm relieved to hear it,' she told him through gritted teeth, finishing trenchantly, 'because you most certainly are not mine.'

'You're overreacting,' she heard Luke saying as he shrugged his shoulders dismissively.

Overreacting? Bobbie could hardly believe her ears.

'You kissed me,' she hissed.

To her chagrin, he actually laughed. 'Oh, come on,' he drawled when he had finished laughing. 'I can't possibly be the first to do that.'

'No,' Bobbie agreed crossly. She just did not believe this; his arrogance almost took her breath away. 'But you're certainly the first who's done so against my will—and the last,' she declared forcefully. For good measure, the memory of his amused laughter driving her on to open retaliation, she added, 'I don't enjoy being kissed by a man I don't like.'

For a moment she finally thought she had got the upper hand, and at six foot plus, Bobbie had to acknowledge that not having it was something of a new experience for her and not one she suspected she could become particularly fond of, but then to her disbelief she heard him drawl, 'No? You could have fooled me. So by whom would you have preferred to be kissed?' he asked before she could react to the enormity of his deliberate insult. 'Or can I guess?' he asked her silkily. 'I saw you watching Max earlier. He's married, you know.'

'Yes, I do know, thank you very much,' Bobbie responded, not bothering to waste time denying his allegations, asking with acid sweetness instead, 'Why, I wonder, is everyone so anxious for me to know that Max is married?'

'You know perfectly well why,' he told her brutally. 'Max is an extremely predatory and highly sexed man, married to a woman who bores him and whom he quite obviously married for reasons that have nothing to do with any urgent need on his part to take her to bed.

'You, on the other hand, possess that peculiar quality that quite obviously does incline Max to want to bed you, but bedding you is all he will do unless, of course, you happen to have a parcel of top-ranking judges, plus a peer and a couple of millionaires tucked away in your family tree.'

'No, I don't,' Bobbie responded shortly, amending mentally for her own benefit, Well, at least I don't have the hereditary peer, but she firmly resisted the temptation to give voice to such words. 'I want you to leave,' she told him quickly instead, looking pointedly towards the door.

'Not yet,' he returned mildly.

Bobbie was completely nonplussed. 'I could ring down to reception and ask them to remove you—forcibly if necessary,' she told him.

Once again he laughed. 'I rather think that in this particular town and this particular hotel, *my* credit and reputation stand rather higher than yours.' One dark brow rose. 'What does anyone know about you after all, other than you appear to have made a rather unlikely friend in Joss?'

'Fenella must be crazy to want to get involved with you,' Bobbie breathed, unwittingly betraying the fact that his past history had been the subject of some of her conversation earlier in the evening. 'And if she's so desperate to get you,' she said bluntly, 'seeing you kissing me isn't going to put her off.'

'No,' he agreed smoothly, 'but hopefully hearing that I've spent the night with you will.'

Spent the night with her? Bobbie's mouth opened and then closed again as she gulped in air and stared at him in a mixture of fury and fascination whilst he watched her back away, one of his eyebrows lifted ironically as though...as though he was almost waiting...enjoying the prospect of having her challenge him. Well, he wasn't going to be disappointed.

'You are *not* staying the night in this room, *my* room,' she emphasised, spacing her words with care.

'No? Then evict me,' Luke responded with a bored shrug.

Evict him. She might be tall, but as she visually measured not just the length of his body, but compared it muscle for muscle, strength for strength, with her own, Bobbie knew that any attempt on her part to use force to remove him from the room would inevitably result in a humiliating failure on her part.

'Very well, then,' Bobbie answered coolly, changing tack. 'If you won't leave, then I shall simply book myself into another room.'

'Impossible, I'm afraid,' Luke told her, shaking his head. 'The hotel is fully booked as I discovered when Fenella announced that she had booked us a double room, but by all means if you want to try...'

Bobbie thought quickly. She was well aware of the curiosity and interest it would arouse if she were to try to change her room, especially with Luke so very much in evidence in her present one.

'This is ridiculous,' she snapped finally. 'If Fenella isn't going to be put off by seeing you kiss me, then what makes you think she will be just because you've spent the night with me? After all, if she's prepared to take on a man who kisses another woman in public, she would more than likely be prepared to take on one who...who's been more intimate with...with her.'

Irritated with herself as she floundered a little, she had no idea why on earth she should feel so self-conscious about using the word 'sex' instead of the more coy and euphemistic 'intimate' in front of a man like Luke

Crighton, a man she didn't so much merely not like, but increasingly actively disliked.

'Because,' Luke explained patiently, 'although *she* might be prepared to do so, she knows perfectly well that *I'm* not.' When Bobbie looked perplexed, he explained matter-of-factly, 'I do *not* sleep around, and as Fenella already knows, I do not and never have been "intimate"—' he underlined the word, her word, mockingly '—with a woman with whom I am not either already involved or intending to become involved in a very serious relationship. In other words, my American friend, Fenella knows that if I spend the night with you, it is because I want to make you a serious and permanent part of my life.'

Bobbie swallowed hard as she stared at him. It wasn't often that anyone caught her wrong-footed or off guard; that anything a member of the male sex said surprised her. But this time...this one...why...why in heaven's name did he have to be the first, the only man she had ever met to echo her own views of the importance of respecting sexual intimacy, to want it to be part of a truly committed relationship?

She gave him a quick glance, half-inclined to suspect him of making fun of her, but one look at his face convinced her that he was totally serious.

'I hope you aren't trying to suggest that because you've forced your way into my room and declared your intention to spend the night with me that that means in the morning you're going to expect me to make an honest man of you,' she joked flippantly to cover what she was feeling.

'Don't you believe in marriage?' he asked her unexpectedly. 'Are you one of these modern young women who likes to think that men are superfluous to her requirements, even to the extent of forgoing the pleasure and the intimacy that creating a child together should bring in favour of a far more clinical and detached method of conception?'

There must be something wrong with her. She must be coming down with some kind of bug, Bobbie decided. There could be no other reason for the sudden flood of heat pouring through her body, the unnerving sensation of weakness and the spine-tingling thrill of shock that had just run through her.

'My plans for the method of conception of my future children is none of your business,' she managed to retort loftily as she fought to control her dizzying light-headedness. She had to get him out of her room and fast, she determined feverishly, but could think of nothing more compelling to say to him other than a decidedly panicky 'You can't sleep here.'

'No,' he agreed unexpectedly as he looked at the bed. 'I can't, and neither, I imagine, can you.' He gave the standard-size hotel bed a disparaging glance. 'If I had to sleep in that toy-box version of what a proper bed should be, I'd wake up with cramp and backache to say the least.'

Bobbie knew exactly what he meant. Back home they had proper beds, big wide long beds in which a person could stretch out luxuriously and still have plenty of room left over for...

A startled glance seized her face, widening her eyes as she absorbed the mental image that had materialised so dangerously out of nowhere—two bodies tangled lovingly together in the comfort of her generously proportioned bed, the fine cotton sheets she favoured wrapped loosely around them, her body snugly protected by the larger, heavier, bulkier form of the man who lay next to her on his side and half across her, one leg flung possessively over her, one arm wrapped securely around her. Little could be seen of his features, but she could visualize the broad, tanned sweep of his well-muscled back and just the beginning of the sensual curve where its line ran into his butt, the dark sleekness of the back of his head, but she knew totally, of course, just what his face looked like, just as she knew, too, how he felt, how he smelled and how he tasted...before love and after it...

She definitely must be ill, Bobbie decided as she finally managed to close her eyes and blink the awesomely realistic vision away. Why else would she be picturing herself in bed with Luke Crighton? And not just any bed, if you please, but her very own bed back home in her small, pretty clapboard house tucked away on one of the quieter streets of their little New England town.

'You can't stay here,' she repeated. Her body trembled as she heard the rusty note of shock in her voice.

'No, I don't think I can,' she heard Luke agreeing. There was an odd note in his voice, as well, but when she looked at him he was focusing on the bed. To her relief he started to walk towards the door, but before he opened it he stopped and turned round saying, 'By the way, exactly how did you come to meet young Joss?'

'I bumped into him by accident in Haslewich,' Bobbie told him truthfully.

'Mmm, so he said,' Luke commented. 'In the churchyard apparently. He said you were looking at the gravestones...?'

Bobbie could feel her heartbeat increasing, the adrenalin starting to pump through her veins as she reacted to her awareness of danger. 'Yes, I was,' she agreed carefully.

'Looking for one in particular?' Luke questioned.

'Just looking,' Bobbie answered. 'As an American I find it's still something of a novelty for me to see gravestones with such old dates on them.'

'You were in the modern part of the graveyard when he saw you, according to Joss.'

'Was I? I can't remember,' Bobbie lied disinterestedly, dropping her head so that her hair swung forward to conceal and protect her expression from him. 'Have you finished your cross-examination?' she asked him with acid sweetness. 'I would like to get some sleep....'

'In order for me to need to cross-question you, you would either have to be guilty of or a witness to some sort of crime,' Luke told her silkily. 'Which, I wonder, did you have in mind when you made that rather betraying statement, and why?'

'Neither,' Bobbie fibbed fiercely as he opened the door and walked through it, but despite the conviction she had injected into her denial, she somehow had the uncomfortable feeling that he didn't believe her.

Oh, damn the man, he was the last complication she needed to have around now, the *very* last.

CHAPTER FOUR

BOBBIE woke up with a start to realise that someone was knocking discreetly on her door. Whoever it was, it thankfully could not possibly be Luke Crighton; discretion and that man could never be said to go hand in hand.

The waiter standing outside with a table fully set for a breakfast for two, which included freshly made Buck's Fizz, refused to listen to her insistence that she had most certainly not ordered such a lavish and highly obvious 'the morning after the night before' breakfast.

'This breakfast was most definitely ordered for this room,' he informed her.

'It can't possibly have been...' Bobbie began to deny and then changed her mind, an ominous thought occurring to her as she demanded warily, 'Ordered by whom?'

'I'm afraid I don't know,' the waiter apologised, but Bobbie suspected that *she* did.

No doubt this was another of Luke Crighton's little tricks to convince Fenella that he had spent the night here with her, although how on earth he expected the other woman to discover that he had ordered breakfast for two for Bobbie's room, she had no idea, unless Fenella was the type who made a habit of checking up on that kind of thing. Perhaps she did. Bobbie made a small moue of distaste before surveying the feast she had been left with. Buck's Fizz... Strong coffee was her normal breakfast indulgence. Somehow she had never seen herself as the kind of woman who drank Buck's Fizz for breakfast and neither, she suspected, did Luke Crighton, not for a moment.

Recklessly she reached for a glass and took a sip. The

orange juice was freshly squeezed and deliciously tangy, the champagne icy cold, making her taste buds shiver in pleasure.

If she had been sharing this treat with a lover, she doubted that it would have done anything to encourage her to leave the warmth of her bed—or him—rather the opposite.

Disconcertingly, just as she raised the glass to her lips to take a second rebellious sip, she was revisited by the same disturbing mental image of Luke she had had the previous evening.

The bubbles in the champagne made her splutter slightly, which just went to show how highly dangerous it could be to consume alcohol first thing in the morning, she told herself sternly, firmly replacing the glass.

An hour later, having consumed two cups of strong coffee and eaten some wholemeal toast, she was downstairs in the hotel lobby comfortably dressed in a pair of soft, cream trousers and a soft, silky knit top.

She wasn't here in England to waste time lying in bed and drinking champagne, she reminded herself firmly, and she certainly wasn't here to indulge in crazy mental images of disconcerting and recklessly intimate scenarios between her and a man who she had good reason to know was never likely to partner her in the kind of highly sensual and erotic love play their tangled bodies had indicated. She walked determinedly across to the reception desk and asked the clerk behind the counter if there were any messages for her.

Smilingly he handed her a couple of sealed notes. Frowning a little since she didn't recognise the handwriting on either of them, Bobbie opened the top one and then dropped it on the desk as though it had burned her fingertips when she read the message contained inside.

'Thank you for last night, you were wonderful. I can't

wait until tonight, Luke.' As the clerk picked up the note and discreetly handed it back to her, Bobbie realised that she was now not the only one to have seen his outrageous message.

He certainly believed in acting out the part, she acknowledged wrathfully as she stuffed the note into her pocket and started to walk away from the reception desk. She opened the other envelope. Its contents, too, were unexpected, but in a very different way from the message contained in Luke's.

It was signed by Olivia and read:

I tried to catch you before we left, but unfortunately we missed you. There is something I would like to discuss with you following our chat last night and I wonder if you are likely to be free to have lunch with me today? If so, could we meet at the Brasserie here at one o'clock?

Olivia

Pensive, Bobbie worried at her bottom lip. She knew, of course, what it was Olivia wanted to discuss; she knew, too, how Sam would feel if she turned down such a golden opportunity. Working for Olivia would give her a good chance to put their plan, or rather Sam's plan, into action. There was no doubt that Olivia would be a valuable contact, but she had liked her so much last night…enjoyed her company and that of her husband so much that she…

She had nothing to lose by at least listening to Olivia, she reminded herself, and potentially an awful lot to gain and not just a free lunch! No, not if she discounted her own sense of honesty and, of course, Olivia's respect and burgeoning friendship….

'Will you be in for lunch?' the receptionist asked her when Bobbie handed in her room key.

'I…yes, I'm lunching with…a friend in the Brasserie at one,' Bobbie told her. There, she had made her decision, committed herself.

As she walked out of the hotel and into the bright sunshine, she wondered if Joss and his family were already on their way back home to Haslewich.

Joss… It was odd to think of him and Max being brothers.

She spent an hour wandering around the town, pausing every now and again to consult her guidebook and admire the city's ancient buildings. Outside the castle she stopped a little longer than she had done anywhere else and even longer outside the building facing onto the river that had a discreet brass plate by the door bearing the legend, 'Crighton, Crighton and Crighton'.

A flutter of movement at an upstairs window made her glance around uneasily and then walk past. Surely there was no one actually working in the offices on a Sunday.

It was half an hour, spent lazily and apparently purposelessly meandering through the narrow streets on a route she had planned earlier, before she arrived at her real destination.

Chester's cathedral had originally and uniquely been a monastery, only later being converted into a church, but fascinating though the history of the building was, Bobbie didn't have time to follow the other tourists in the direction of the ancient arched crypts but instead hurried eagerly in the direction of the graveyard.

It didn't take long to find what she was looking for. In Chester the Crightons had been men of substance and law for many, many generations as the large mausoleum in which they had chosen to bury their dead testified.

Bobbie gazed at it with mixed feelings. Some of the names inscribed on the marble tablet affixed to one end were so faded it was almost impossible to read them;

others were much brighter, much newer. Unsteadily she reached out and traced one of the names.

'He was my great-grandfather,' a familiarly unwelcome voice said from behind her.

I know, Bobbie wanted to say, and it was his disapproval of his youngest son's marriage that led to the latter leaving home to establish the Haslewich branch of the family with his new wife, but, of course, she said no such thing. She didn't even turn round.

Instead she simply said as levelly and as calmly as she could, 'Luke, what are you doing here?'

'I rather think that question would be more appropriate coming from me to you,' he responded dryly. 'For such a young woman you seem to have developed a rather morbid penchant for visiting graveyards, first in Haslewich and now here in Chester.'

'It's an interesting way of discovering more about the families who lived in the area,' Bobbie returned neutrally, adding more challengingly, 'and it certainly isn't a crime.'

'No, not unless you're planning on exhuming one of the bodies, it isn't,' Luke agreed, stepping forward so that he was standing alongside her, but Bobbie still didn't look directly at him. 'So it's your interest in local history that brings you here, then. Local history in general or more specifically one particular local family?' he asked pointedly.

'I was looking around the cathedral,' Bobbie told him, shrugging her shoulders dismissively. 'I took a wrong turning and found myself out here. This mausoleum caught my eye and I came over to look at it...'

'And by the greatest coincidence, discovered it belonged to the Crightons,' Luke supplied for her. 'You're lying,' he confronted her bluntly, adding before she could speak, 'And don't bother perjuring yourself by denying it. I've been watching you. I saw you stop outside the office. You didn't come out here in error, you—'

'Watching me? You mean you've been following me, spying on me,' Bobbie burst out furiously. 'Back home we have laws against that kind of…of harassment…that kind of pervert,' she raged on forcefully, curling her lip and glaring at him in determined outrage.

'Indeed, well, we all have our own beliefs about what does and what does not constitute violation of privacy. *I don't know* what kind of game you're playing or what you're after, but believe me, I intend to find out,' he warned her grimly, 'and *when* I do…'

'You'll what…use your legal powers to have me thrown in jail? I don't think so,' Bobbie told him scornfully. 'If I were you, instead of persecuting me and worrying about me, I'd be looking into my family tree to see if there's any history of paranoia lurking there because, boy oh boy, are you ever exhibiting some,' Bobbie said even more scathingly, praying that he would put her flushed face and obvious agitation down to anger and not to the sickening sense of guilt and dread that was gripping her.

'I can see you're an aficionado of the cult that believes that attack is the best form of defence,' Luke responded dryly. '*I'm* not a young boy of Joss's age to be beguiled and deceived by a head of blonde hair and a pair of blue eyes, you know,' he told her harshly.

'No,' Bobbie agreed bitingly. 'At least not unless it comes packaged with a simpering smile and is under five-five in height.'

She held her breath as she saw the ominous surge of anger darken his skin and harden his mouth.

'We're getting off the point,' he returned tersely, but as she started to exhale her pent-up breath in a leaky sigh of relief, she quickly realised he had picked up the attack again. 'You still haven't explained why it was *our* family mausoleum that attracted your attention,' he demanded.

'It was simply that I recognised the name,' Bobbie fibbed. 'It caught my eye and I came over to have a look and—'

'You had to walk past four other family vaults to get here.' His brows rose, underlining the cynicism in his voice as he pointed out, 'Something must have made you pick it out.'

'I'm a woman,' Bobbie told him sweetly. 'I never go for the obvious.'

'You could have fooled me,' he replied dryly as he elucidated, 'They don't come much more obvious than Max and last night you couldn't take your eyes off him.'

'He's a very good-looking man,' Bobbie offered carelessly.

'He's also a man with a wife,' Luke reminded her again sharply.

Bobbie frowned as she caught sight of her watch. Twelve-thirty. She ought to start back if she was going to be in time to meet Olivia. 'I have to go,' she told him. 'I have a lunch date.'

Luke was frowning. 'With Max?' he pounced.

'Work it out for yourself, Counsel,' she taunted him, headily relieved that he had stopped cross-questioning her about her interest in the mausoleum.

It had given her a bad shock when she had heard his voice and realised that he was standing behind her, and an even worse one when he had informed her that he had seen her outside the offices, she acknowledged as she stepped back from him and started to walk away, so sure that he would make some attempt to either stop her or follow her that she had to turn around when she had reached the exit just to check where he was.

He was standing with his back to her in front of the family grave, and as she watched, he suddenly knelt down and with very great care, tenderness almost, started to remove the weeds that had rooted in the soft grass around the tomb, so engrossed in his task that she might not even have existed.

Shakily she turned away and started to walk quickly in the direction she had originally come.

She made it back to the Grosvenor with ten minutes to spare, and by the time she returned from her room where she had gone to tidy up and brush her hair, Olivia was waiting for her in the foyer.

'Oh good,' she exclaimed when she saw Bobbie heading towards her. 'I was beginning to think that you weren't going to come.'

'I spent the morning exploring the cathedral,' Bobbie explained, 'and I got back a little later than I'd planned. Your note said that there was something you wanted to discuss with me.'

'Yes,' Olivia agreed as they headed for the Brasserie, obviously a popular place for lunch on a Sunday, Bobbie realised when she saw how full it was.

The *maître d'* still welcomed them warmly, though, as he showed them to their table.

'It's not so much something I wanted to discuss as a proposition I wanted to put to you,' Olivia confessed once they were sitting down and had been handed their menus. 'I mentioned to you last night the problems that Caspar and I are having finding a nanny for Amelia and you said you had some experience with children.'

'Yes,' Bobbie replied cautiously, sensing what was coming. 'You said that Caspar had taken on the role of househusband during the summer vacation.'

'That's right,' Olivia agreed. 'But now, with the new academic year looming, he really needs to get down to some preparatory work. Ruth is marvellous helping out when she can, but it really isn't fair to expect her to do more than the occasional babysit for us.'

'No, I suppose at her age...' Bobbie began, but Olivia shook her head.

'Oh, heavens no, it's got nothing to do with her age. Ruth might have just hit her seventies but she looks more than ten years younger, and so far as her intellectual and energy levels go, she certainly puts me to shame. She's wonderful with children, as well. It's such a shame that she's never had any of her own.'

'Some women just aren't particularly maternal,' Bobbie offered quietly.

'Some aren't,' Olivia concurred as the waiter took their orders and removed the menus, 'but Ruth most certainly is. It's a pity that she never married.'

'Perhaps she never found anyone who could give her enough to compensate for losing her right to call herself a Crighton,' Bobbie suggested.

She could see Olivia giving her a puzzled look.

'It's true that some *male* members of the family do see themselves as coming somewhere just a little below God and most definitely very much higher than anyone else, but Ruth has certainly never held that kind of view. No, I think the fact that she has never married has more to do with the fact that her fiancé—a fighter pilot—was killed during the last war than anything else, although according to Caspar...' Olivia paused, frowned and then without completing her original statement continued, 'Joss absolutely adores her and she thinks the world of him.'

'Because he's a boy...a male,' Bobbie offered dryly.

'No, because he's Joss,' Olivia told her firmly. 'We seem to have given you a rather off-putting view of her. I don't know how. She really is the most wonderful person...caring...understanding...and very wise somehow.' She gave a tiny shake of her head.

'I'm letting myself get rather sidetracked.' She smiled at the waiter who had brought their food, then waited until he had gone before continuing quietly, 'Caspar and I were wondering, since you said you'd planned to stay in the area for a while, if you would consider coming to work for us on a part-time basis to keep an eye on Amelia so that Caspar can get on with some work. You needn't worry that you'd be left in full-time charge of her—Caspar will still be based at home.'

Bobbie put down her fork, the food on it uneaten. 'I don't know what to say... I haven't really got the experience....'

'You *did* say at Katie and Louise's birthday party that you'd worked at a local crèche in the holidays,' Olivia reminded her.

Bobbie nodded her head. 'Yes,' she admitted slowly, 'but that was a nursery for children with special needs, older children who needed special trained help,' she emphasised. 'I, we...I was just there to fetch and carry, really.'

The way Olivia was watching her made her feel slightly embarrassed and she wished now she hadn't mentioned the voluntary work she had done as a teenager, following in a family tradition that made it natural and instinctive for her to want to help others less advantaged than she was herself.

'There aren't any small children in our close family,' she felt she had to point out to Olivia, 'and I'd be lying to you if I said anything other than I don't really have the remotest idea of what it's like to have sole responsibility of a very young child.'

'You won't be expected to—at least not on your own,' Olivia assured her promptly. 'As I said, Caspar will be there and I promise you that not only is he a dab hand at changing nappies and giving bottles, much better than I am myself if I'm honest,' she admitted ruefully, 'but he's also the type of doting father who actually enjoys doing so.

'No, it's simply a matter of your being there so that Caspar can work in peace. I'm afraid a lot of the time it will probably be quite boring for you. She doesn't do much at this stage apart from eating and sleeping, although Caspar is convinced that she's already showing early signs of having inherited his intelligence.'

They both laughed.

'I…how long would you need me for?' Bobbie asked hesitantly. It wasn't, after all, what she had planned and would certainly curtail her freedom, her ability to come and go as she chose, but there was no doubt that it would also put her in a very advantageous position when it came to…

'Four weeks, possibly six,' Olivia told her hopefully.

'I'm really not sure that I'd be the right person.…' Bobbie hedged, her emotional misgivings surfacing.

'Yes, you are,' Olivia reassured her firmly. 'I know it sounds a silly thing for me to say, especially with my legal training,' she added ruefully, 'but from the moment we met I felt…' She paused and gave Bobbie a wry look. 'I'm not normally given to bold pronouncements and vague utterances about instinct and the like, but all I can say is that I felt so instantly at home and comfortable with you almost in a way as though you were family that I know that Amelia will feel the same, and Caspar agrees with me.'

'That's some compliment,' Bobbie admitted shakily as she felt her eyes blur slightly with emotional tears. 'I'm not sure I can live up to it.…'

'Of course you can,' Olivia countered robustly. 'And look, if it makes you feel more comfortable, why don't we agree on a week's trial on either side, which would give us both the option to back out gracefully if we should feel the need? You did say that you needed to earn some money,' Olivia reminded her.

Yes, she realised she had said that and there was no

doubt that taking the job Olivia had so unexpectedly offered her had many advantages, not the least the fact that she would now have a completely legitimate reason for remaining in the area.

'I…look, can I think about it and tell you tomorrow?' she asked Olivia.

'Tonight,' Olivia stressed determinedly.

'Tonight,' Bobbie agreed with a smile.

'Good…now there's just one more thing,' Olivia said, pushing back her chair. 'Would you excuse me for a moment?'

'Of course,' Bobbie replied. No doubt Olivia was going to telephone Caspar to tell him how their interview had gone, she decided, but five minutes later when Olivia returned, her face wreathed in smiles and carrying a small bundle wreathed in blankets, Bobbie knew that she had guessed wrong.

'Meet your new charge-to-be,' Olivia announced, unceremoniously placing the bundle in Bobbie's arms.

Just for a second her first reaction was to reject it…her…thrust her away, but then the baby opened her eyes and Bobbie's heart caught in a painful lunge of recognition as she looked down into the tiny baby features and instinct took over from caution and she was holding Amelia tightly in her arms, cooing inanities and breathing in the delicious baby smell and hopelessly, desperately, falling head over heels in love with her.

The difficulty was not going to be whether she could take to Olivia and Caspar's baby, she acknowledged shakily, but whether she could bear to let Amelia go!

'She's beautiful,' she told Olivia huskily.

Olivia gave her a pleased maternal smile. 'We certainly think so,' she said, 'although it is quite unusual in this family to have a redhead, and as for those eyes…'

'It's something to do with the combination of dark and fair genes,' Bobbie explained absently. 'It sometimes produces this particular colouring apparently—dark red hair and sea green eyes.'

'Yes, Aunt Ruth said much the same thing,' Olivia agreed, exclaiming happily, 'Oh look, Luke's just come in,' and standing up, she waved him over before Bobbie could say or do anything.

As they waited for him to weave his way towards them through the busy room, Olivia confided to Bobbie, 'At least he seems to have shaken Fenella off at last, thank goodness. There was a moment when we began to think she was going to manage to manoeuvre him into taking her back. That woman is a positive leech and Luke is such a softy at heart. Mind you,' she added coyly, 'I rather suspect that the two of *you* are on much better terms than you want the rest of us to believe.' She explained knowingly, 'I saw that he'd left you a note when I left mine. I recognised his handwriting.'

Bobbie's heart sank. This was a development she *hadn't* anticipated and certainly didn't feel equipped to cope with. 'Olivia, you don't understand,' she started to protest.

But Olivia simply gave her a mischievous smile and shook her head, telling her, 'You don't have to explain to me. I *can* still remember how it feels when you first fall in love.'

Fall in love! This was terrible! Dreadful! But before she could say anything more, Luke reached them.

'Luke,' Olivia exclaimed fondly as he leaned down to kiss her cheek before taking a seat.

Bobbie saw his eyebrows lift as he glanced at her, his gaze sharpening as he saw that she was holding Amelia.

'It's all right. Your god-daughter's in perfectly good hands,' Olivia teased him, adding, 'so good in fact that we're hoping to persuade Bobbie to keep on holding her.'

'Oh?' Luke questioned, looking sombrely from Bobbie to Olivia.

'Yes,' Olivia continued easily, patently unaware of the undercurrent of dislike and hostility emanating from Luke to her, which Bobbie was so keenly conscious of. 'Caspar and I have asked Bobbie if she would be willing to stay on in the area for a few more weeks to take care of Amelia so that Caspar can get some work done prior to the start of the new term.'

'I thought you already had a qualified nanny,' Luke returned sharply, emphasising the word 'qualified'.

'We did,' Olivia agreed.

'I really must go,' Bobbie announced, getting up ready to hand the baby back to her mother, but before she could do so, Luke, too, stood up, firmly removing Amelia from her arms and standing so close to her whilst he did so that she could actually smell the scent of his skin—and his body....

The baby gurgled delightfully up at him, a huge smile curling her mouth.

'You can tell she's going to be a man's woman,' Olivia said, laughing fondly as she, too, got to her feet. 'I'll ring you later...about seven,' she told Bobbie as she walked with her towards the exit. Then unexpectedly Olivia reached out and gave Bobbie a swift hug. 'Oh, please don't say no,' she pleaded. 'I know you're going to be just right, and by the way, I forgot to say, you can live in with us if that's convenient for you. You'd have your own room and bathroom, but if you prefer not to, then that's equally fine.'

Bobbie had just got as far as the bank of lifts that gave access to the upper floors of the hotel when she heard Luke calling her name with crisp firmness. Suppressing a childish urge to pretend she hadn't heard him and step into the lift that had temptingly opened, she turned round.

His 'I want a word with you,' instead of intimidating her as she suspected he had intended, made her straighten her spine and draw herself up to her full height, an impressive and, to some men she knew, an awesome sight, not one that sat well with their vulnerable male egos. However, it was obvious that Luke was not exactly impressed, but then of course, she did still have to tilt her chin just that betraying little bit extra in order to look into his eyes.

'Why did you let me think that you were having lunch with Max?' he asked her without preamble.

'*I let* you think?' Bobbie queried dryly.

'You know what I mean,' he flung back curtly. 'You were perfectly aware of what I thought but you didn't correct my misconception.'

'Didn't I?' Bobbie asked him dulcetly, and then seeing that they were beginning to attract the interested and amused attention of a small group of people waiting to step into the adjacent lift, she told him quickly and quietly, 'Whom I do or do not choose to have lunch with is no business of yours.'

'Max is a married man,' he reminded her grittily.

'And so you keep saying, and for all you know *I* may very well be a married woman,' Bobbie retaliated.

'What?'

The look in his eyes as he stepped forward and took hold of her upper arm, drawing her back out of earshot of anyone else and into the partially secluded shadows of the corridor, gave her such a shock that she actually felt physically weak and light-headed.

'*Are* you married?' she heard him demanding.

'No,' Bobbie admitted shakily.

She had heard of people going weak with fear and even with nervousness but to actually feel this intense sense of physical dizziness simply because of the way a man was looking at her... A phrase she had heard a girlfriend use once and at the time teased her for suddenly came back to her.

'He makes me feel quite literally weak with lust,' she had said.

Weak with lust—her—for a man whom she positively disliked. Never. Impossible. She must be imagining things, getting her signals all mixed up.

'Do you intend to accept this job that Olivia's offered you?' she heard Luke asking her abruptly.

'I don't know, I haven't made up my mind yet. Why are you asking me all these questions?' she asked him defensively, wishing that her voice didn't sound quite so vulnerable and breathless and that her heart wasn't beating quite so betrayingly fast.

He had released her arm now but he was still standing very close to her, and to her chagrin, she could actually feel her body reacting to the proximity of him. Thank the Lord she was wearing a jacket, because there was simply no way she could have passed off the sudden burgeoning of her nipples as a mere automatic reaction to an adverse change in temperature, and she knew that if Luke could see what she was feeling, he would be as aware as she was herself of what was happening to her.

He still hadn't answered her question but as she started to look past him, back towards the lifts, he told her bluntly, 'Well, let's just say I'm following the same line of investigation as when I asked why you had a penchant for visiting graveyards.'

Bobbie could feel the anxious tension starting to churn her stomach. 'Look,' she told him huskily, 'that was just a coincidence.'

'So you said earlier,' he agreed, 'but not, I have to say, very convincingly.'

'What are you trying to suggest?' Bobbie demanded,

hoping that he couldn't tell just how nervous and guilty he was making her feel.

'Nothing,' he replied, but before she could draw a shaky breath of relief, he added warningly, 'as yet. Let's just say that I'm holding a watching brief.'

'It's Fenella you should be watching and not me,' Bobbie advised as she quickly stepped away from him and darted into the lift. She reached out to press the button and then tensed as he followed her and placed his hand against the door, preventing it from closing.

'I rather suspect that in comparison to you, any element of danger that Fenella might represent would be minimal indeed,' he parried.

'That's your expert opinion as a barrister, is it?' Bobbie quipped flippantly.

'No, that's my gut instinct as a man,' he told her cynically.

She removed his hand from the door and it slid shut before Bobbie could come up with any suitable reply.

Once she had gained the relative sanctuary of her room and double bolted the door, Bobbie picked up the telephone receiver and punched in her parents' New England home number, keeping her fingers crossed that it would be her sister who answered her call and not her mother.

Fortunately it was. 'Sam...?'

'Yes, it's me,' her twin affirmed unnecessarily, adding, 'You sound a mite out of breath. Anything wrong?'

'Nooo...' Bobbie denied unconvincingly, then asked anxiously, 'How are things back there?'

Their mother had been advised by her gynaecologist to have a hysterectomy some time ago, and whether as a result of this or because of her having hit fifty, in the months since the operation she had suffered from uncharacteristic bouts of a troubling depression.

She was over the worst now and they were not to

worry, nor were they to pamper her or indulge her fool-
ishness, she had insisted to both her daughters and her
husband, but all three of them were very much aware of
the shadowed sadness in her eyes and the unfamiliar
droop of her mouth when she thought that no one was
watching her.

'So so,' Samantha replied guardedly. 'The folks are
still down in Washington but they're due back tomorrow. I spoke to Dad last night and he said they'd both
be glad to get home. I guess he's thinking that he may
not run for office next time around. He thinks it might
be too stressful for Mom.'

'Oh, Sam,' Bobbie protested.

'I know,' her elder twin sympathised, asking her,
'How are you getting on?'

'I...I'm not sure,' Bobbie told her hesitantly. 'You
remember I told you about the party I was invited to?
Well, one of the other guests, a member of the family,
invited me out to lunch today to ask me if I'd like a
temporary job with them, looking after their baby, but—'

She stopped speaking as her sister interrupted her excitedly, saying, 'Wow, that's wonderful, just the kind of
break we needed. You'll be able to—'

'Sam. I'm not so sure that I... I like Olivia,' she tried
to explain hesitantly to her sister, who had suddenly
gone ominously quiet, wishing as she had wished so
often over these past few days that Samantha were here
with her. 'She's so genuine...so kind, and I feel—'

'You *like* her?' Samantha questioned fiercely.
'Bobbie—Roberta—have you forgotten who she
is...who they are,' she demanded insistently, 'what they
did?'

'No...of course I haven't. It's just...I hate to be de-
ceitful like this, Sam, and—'

'This is no time to go all soft-hearted,' Samantha told

her sister assertively. 'Look, I've got to go. Ring me tomorrow.'

After she had replaced the receiver, Samantha stood staring out of the window of her parents' handsome drawing room at the empty drive outside. The creeper-clad, solidly built New England mansion was one of the finest examples of late eighteenth-century buildings in the area. It had originally been built by one of their father's ancestors and in due course would pass on into the ownership of their brother Tom, now presently at Harvard, but it was not the thought of her younger brother ultimately inheriting the house in which both she and Bobbie had grown up that was causing a deep frown to crease her forehead.

'I knew I should have gone to England,' she muttered under her breath. 'Bobbie never did have much of a stomach for fighting dirty.'

It was she who had masterminded the plan they were now putting into action, she who had been the driving force behind it, and unlike Bobbie, she who knew she would never have fallen into the trap of 'liking' those cussed and accursed Crightons, as the twins had grown into the habit of calling them when they had inadvertently stumbled on the secret that their mother had found so shameful that she hadn't wanted them to know about.

It had been their grandfather in the end who had answered their questions. And even now, although they were adult and had known the story for many years, their mother still did not like to talk about it or hear it mentioned because it still hurt her so much, all the more so, Samantha suspected, because of their father's very distinguished and strait-laced Puritan ancestry.

Not that knowing the truth made their father love their mother any the less, nor did they, but it still hurt to see her vulnerable.

'It's not fair. Why should Mom be the only one to

suffer?' Samantha had demanded of Bobbie. 'It wasn't her fault. We should make them pay.'

'But how can we?' Bobbie had asked her.

'I'll think of a way,' Samantha had promised.

And so she had…or rather she had thought she had until Bobbie started to turn chicken-hearted.

If only she wasn't committed to her college classes and her vow to make up for the time she had taken off to travel. Still, there was no point in regretting that now; she would just have to make sure that Bobbie didn't weaken still further.

In Chester, Bobbie paced her bedroom unhappily. She just didn't possess Sam's fiercely stubborn determination and adherence to any cause she took on; she lacked her sister's strength, she knew that. It wasn't that she cared any the less about their mother. It was just…

Face it, she told herself sternly, you're a coward. You just can't abide any kind of fighting or confrontation. You're a real scaredy-cat, she taunted herself.

But what was she so afraid of? Seeing the friendship and warmth in Olivia's and Joss's eyes turn to dislike and contempt when they discovered how devious and underhand she had been, or seeing the triumph in Luke's when all his suspicions of her were confirmed?

CHAPTER FIVE

WHEN Olivia rang later in the day as she had promised she would, Bobbie took a deep breath and made a fervent mental plea that she was making the right decision as she confirmed that she wanted to accept her offer of a job.

'You'll do it! Oh, that's wonderful!' Olivia enthused, adding, 'I was so afraid that you were going to say no.'

Bobbie bit her lip as she prayed that Olivia would never have cause to wish that she had refused whilst she listened to her explain the finer details of their arrangement.

'Oh, and don't worry about transport,' she told Bobbie. 'We'll provide you with a car. You'll certainly need one because we are rather isolated, I'm afraid.'

Well, at least that solved the problem of how she was going to explain away being able to afford the cost of a hire-car, Bobbie acknowledged as Olivia went on to detail the generous amount of time off she would be given plus the use of the car for her personal needs.

It was agreed that Olivia would pick her up at the hotel in the morning, but despite the other woman's enthusiasm, Bobbie was not surprised to discover that her hand was shaking and her stomach churning with nauseous apprehension when she finally replaced the receiver.

Still, at least there was a positive advantage to leaving Chester—she would not be likely to see Luke Crighton again.

'I've told Joss that you might be coming to work for us,' Olivia had informed her. 'He's thrilled to bits!'

* * *

Bobbie spent the rest of the evening packing her things and trying to ignore the sad little voice of her conscience.

After all, how could she have faced her twin sister if she had refused such a golden opportunity? And, given the choice, she would much rather confront and deal with her own conscience than Sam's ire!

'Here we are, home safe and sound,' Olivia announced with a smile as she drove in between the gateposts towards the pretty low-roofed brick building that was her home and that, as she had already explained to Bobbie, had originally been a small block of three farm workers' cottages.

'They came up for auction along with a couple of paddocks just before we got married. It was Luke who tipped us off about them. He knew it was exactly the kind of place we were looking for—something large enough in which to bring up a family and with a good bit of land, but nothing too grand or expensive.

'For the first six months we owned it, the place was completely uninhabitable, and we were still virtually knee-deep in builders and decorators and the like when Amelia was born.'

'It looks wonderful,' Bobbie enthused as she gazed appreciatively at the neatly painted windows and the mellow warmth of the old bricks.

'Come on,' Olivia instructed her as she stopped the car. 'Let's go in. Caspar is dying for you to arrive.'

'I hope I'm not going to let you down.' Bobbie hesitated. 'I...I really don't know that much about babies or small children.'

'Neither did I until I had Amelia,' Olivia confessed cheerfully. 'She liked you,' she added warmly. 'I could see that, and quite frankly that's much more important to me than a long string of qualifications. Mmm...I'm surprised that Caspar hasn't come out to welcome you.'

Uncertainly, Bobbie followed Olivia as she led her, not to the prettily painted front door of the now-amalgamated cottages but around the side of the house and through a gate into a walled courtyard area and towards what Bobbie guessed must be the back door.

As Bobbie followed her through it into the kitchen, she heard Olivia exclaim, 'Ruth! I didn't realise you were here!' Bobbie followed Olivia's gaze and saw an elegantly dressed, serenely attractive woman whose still dark, well-styled hair made her look nothing like the age that Bobbie knew her to be.

If Ruth's clothes and supple, slender body looked elegant, the pose she had adopted on the floor where she was obviously playing with Olivia's baby daughter most certainly was not. Her carelessly sprawled body and the warm, rich uninhibited sound of her laughter surely belonged more to a girl in her late teens or early twenties rather than a woman of such maturity, Bobbie decided, her own body stiffening slightly in a mixture of wariness and covert disdain as Ruth scrambled to her feet, still laughing as she explained, 'Caspar had to go out—an urgent meeting. He phoned and asked me if I could come over.'

'Oh, Ruth, we impose on you far too much,' Olivia apologised as she hugged her great-aunt warmly, 'but not, I promise you, any more. This is Bobbie. She's going to be looking after Amelia for us for a few weeks to give us time to find a more permanent nanny.'

If Ruth Crighton's demeanour and body language seemed surprisingly youthful, then the look of extraordinary wisdom and kindness in her eyes told a very different story, Bobbie acknowledged, shaken by the unexpectedness of the emotions that overwhelmed her as Ruth held out her hand towards her. Her first instinct was to step back from her to avoid any kind of physical contact with her. But her mother had had an old-fashioned attitude towards teaching her children good manners and Bobbie found that she was automatically extending her own hand.

Ruth's clasp was firm but feminine, the bones in her hand fine and delicate. Bobbie had to look away and blink frantically in case the sudden rush of tears to her eyes betrayed her. The feel of that elegantly shaped, long-fingered hand with its smooth, delicate, English-rose skin was almost unbearably familiar.

'I've been looking forward to meeting you,' she heard Ruth telling her warmly before adding, 'Joss drew a most intriguing verbal picture of you.'

'I suppose he told you that I was a giant.' Bobbie smiled back, taking refuge from her own chaotic emotions in making a joke about her height.

'Actually, no, he didn't,' Ruth denied. 'He told me that you liked reading tombstones and that you were just the right height for Luke.'

To her own dismay, Bobbie realised that she was actually blushing.

'He also said that you were American and that he liked you,' Ruth added with another smile, tactfully ignoring Bobbie's embarrassment.

American *and* he liked her or American *but* he liked her? Bobbie wondered as her self-consciousness subsided and she was unable to stop herself from asking dryly, 'I see. Does that mean that normally the two aren't found to be compatible?'

Ruth's eyebrows rose, her fine eyes rather thoughtful as she studied Bobbie's face. There was no doubt that the American was a vibrantly beautiful young woman. Ruth could see intelligence as well as pride in her expression, but even more intriguingly she could also see an unexpected hint of uncertainty and defensiveness.

'Oh dear,' Olivia broke in ruefully. 'I suspect that must mean that Joss has been telling you tales about how certain members of the Crighton clan have in the past been chauvinistically anti-American. I can remember how shocked I was when Caspar told me that he'd heard about it, but that's all in the past now, Bobbie,' she said reassuringly. 'If it ever really existed.'

'There was a certain amount of local resentment and male jealousy of the American forces stationed here during the Second World War,' Ruth supplied quietly, 'but that was all a long time ago and I believe what ill feeling there may have been has been exaggerated into a bit of a shaggy-dog story.'

'Mmm... Uncle Jon seems to feel that it was your father who first started the whole anti-American thing,' Olivia commented. 'Something about some argument he'd had with someone in authority on the American side...'

Bobbie wondered if she was being over-sensitive in thinking that Ruth hesitated just that little bit too long before replying and that her voice was not quite so naturally or warmly pitched as it had been before as she responded, 'That may very well have been the case. Your great-grandfather had his own very decided views on things and he certainly wasn't too happy with the way the Ministry had appropriated land—especially when it was *his* land—for war use and I believe there were certain quarrels and petty arguments over his belief that he still had a right to walk on what he considered to be his own land while the authorities viewed that he was trespassing on what was now military property.'

Olivia laughed and, as she bent down to scoop up her small daughter who was now beginning to object to the lack of adult attention, told Bobbie, 'Well, you can rest assured, Bobbie, that Americans are more than welcome in this household. You will stay for lunch, won't you?'

she turned to ask Ruth as the older woman started to straighten her skirt.

'I wish I could, but it's the Simmonds' wedding this weekend and I promised I'd help with the flowers for the church today,' Ruth answered, turning away from Olivia and smiling gently at Bobbie as she added, 'It's been lovely to meet you. Perhaps Olivia will bring you over to see me before you leave.'

'Bring her over to see you... How formal.' Olivia pulled a face.

Without waiting for Bobbie to reply, Ruth turned back to her small great-great-niece, her eyes alight with tenderness and love as she bent her head to kiss her.

'Ruth is wonderful with children,' Olivia told Bobbie ten minutes later after Ruth had driven off.

'Yes...yes, I can see that she is,' Bobbie agreed flatly. The day had suddenly started to turn sour on her. She had the beginnings of what promised to be a very bad headache, and for the first time since she had come to Britain, she missed her twin so much that she positively ached with the pain of wanting her.

'Bobbie, what is it? Are you feeling all right?' Olivia asked her anxiously. 'You weren't upset by what we were saying about Americans, were you? It was thoughtless of me to bring it up. It's just that you're almost bound to meet Gramps and, well, depending on what kind of mood he's in and how much his hip is paining him, he can be rather...tactless. He's rather behind the times, I'm afraid, and his outlook is very blinkered. You'd never believe that he and Ruth are brother and sister. She's so modern and so forward-thinking. I know that Gramps is older than her but sometimes you'd think he's got stuck in some kind of time warp, whereas Ruth—'

'You obviously think very highly of her,' Bobbie commented abruptly.

Olivia gave her a thoughtful look.

'Yes...yes...I do,' she agreed gravely. 'You see... Well, let's just say that if it wasn't for Ruth, I doubt very much that Caspar and I would be together today and I certainly wouldn't have you, would I, my wonderful, precious, naughty little one?' She smiled, hugging her gurgling daughter.

'In many ways, Ruth and Jon's wife, Jenny, have been the true mother figures in my life, the people I've turned to for help and advice and, yes, for the definition of myself as a woman. My own mother...' She gave Bobbie a sad look. 'It's no secret and you're bound to hear about it sooner or later, so I may as well tell you myself. My mother, Tania, suffered very badly from...from an eating disorder. So badly, in fact, that even now, although she's in recovery, she still needs help.'

'Oh, I'm so sorry,' Bobbie commiserated, genuinely moved to compassion, not just for Olivia but for her unknown mother, as well.

'Yes, so am I,' Olivia agreed, 'which is just one of the reasons why I'm so determined that this little madam gets a very different kind of mothering.'

'And your father?' Bobbie asked hesitantly.

'Who knows?' Olivia returned dryly. 'He...he disappeared shortly after my mother became ill—he'd been recovering from a heart attack in a nursing home and he just walked out. We've tried to find him but...'

'And you've heard nothing from him?' Bobbie asked her, shocked.

'Two postcards, one from Italy and the other from South America, but we still haven't been able to trace him.' Olivia gave a small shrug.

'As Amelia grows up, Jenny and Jon will be her maternal grandparents and Ruth... Ruth, I hope, will always be Amelia's special person and be there for her as she was for me when I was a child and as she is now for Joss. She's convinced that, of all of us, he's the one who will fulfil all of Gramps's ambitions, and she's probably right. Mind you, Joss is going to have a long way to go before he matches Luke's awesome courtroom manner,' Olivia noted, smiling.

'Yes. I can imagine,' Bobbie agreed grimly. 'He must be a ruthless prosecutor.'

'Prosecutor!' Olivia stared at her. 'Oh, but Luke specialises in defence, didn't he tell you? That's his forte.'

'Whom does he defend?' Bobbie muttered cynically, trying not to betray her discomfort. 'Murderers and rapists?'

She could see from Olivia's expression that she had gone too far and inwardly cursed her runaway tongue's impulsiveness.

'I'm sorry,' she apologised guiltily. 'It's just...'

'It's all right,' Olivia assured her. 'You don't have to explain to me. Caspar and I had some pretty horrendous fights in our time.'

Whilst Bobbie stared at her, she added illuminatingly, 'I'm afraid that Fenella wasn't too discreet in giving vent to her feelings about discovering the pair of you together. I don't intend to pry,' she declared firmly. 'But, well, let's just say that it's pretty obvious that there's a certain something smouldering away between you, and my experience is that when something smoulders, sparks can fly,' Olivia finished more light-heartedly.

Bobbie didn't say a word. How could she? She was too busy trying to grapple with the latest complication in her life. She doubted that Luke would be too pleased at discovering that at least one member of his extended family and possibly others appeared to think that they were something of an 'item'. Well, he only had himself to blame, and unpleasant though she might find the thought of being linked romantically to him, *she* at least would soon be walking away from the situation—and from him.

For now, though, she was caught in something of a cleft stick. She either allowed Olivia to continue thinking that there *was* some kind of romance going on between herself and Luke or she told her that there wasn't and left her believing that she had simply spent the night with him. Of the two, the second option was certainly the more unpalatable, Bobbie acknowledged, and besides, she rather suspected that Luke would find it much more difficult to explain his way out of a supposed romance than to dismiss a mere one-night stand, and if he was busy doing that, he would surely have far less time to indulge his suspicions of her. In fact, the more Bobbie thought about it, the more advantages she could see in allowing the fiction that she and Luke were attracted to one another to continue.

For a start, it would allow her to be far more openly curious about Luke's family background than she could allow herself to be as a mere substitute nanny and for another thing... Well, she admitted that she wouldn't have been human if she wasn't enjoying the prospect of seeing Luke wrong-footed and discomforted and she certainly knew exactly how *he* would feel at the idea of having her for a 'girlfriend'.

And then another thought struck her.

'I hope you didn't offer me this job because...because of me and Luke,' she asked Olivia uncomfortably.

'Certainly not,' Olivia reassured her immediately. 'No, Caspar and I had already talked about approaching you on the night of the party. Which reminds me, could you hold Amelia for a moment, please, while I go and ring Caspar and find out what time he's coming home?'

Left alone with her new charge, Bobbie smilingly returned the baby's curious, round-eyed stare, enjoying the soft, warm feel of her in her arms, and instinctively started to talk to her.

When Olivia returned, Amelia was smiling hugely in Bobbie's arms whilst Bobbie herself...

Some women just had a natural mothering instinct, Olivia believed, and Bobbie, whether she knew it yet or not, was definitely one of them.

Twenty-four hours later, even Bobbie herself was surprised at how easily she had fitted into the household. Caspar and Olivia treated her more as a friend than an employee, and as for Amelia...

She was delicious, Bobbie had happily and wholeheartedly told a grinning Caspar. Yummy, delicious, delectable and definitely the most intelligent and aware eight-month-old who had ever existed.

'You're almost as bad as Luke,' Olivia teasingly scolded her later that evening. 'He's the most besotted godfather that ever was.'

'And a far better choice than Saul would have been,' Caspar chipped in, adding dryly, '*He* would have been more interested in making eyes at Amelia's mother than at Amelia.'

'Caspar!' Olivia warned him.

'Saul's my father's cousin,' she explained to Bobbie. 'You may have met him at the birthday party.'

'He was the one Louise was desperately trying to impress,' Caspar supplied helpfully, 'but she's wasting her time because Saul—'

'Caspar...' Olivia warned a little more firmly this time. 'Saul's much too old for Louise,' she explained. 'He's well into his thirties now and Louise is only eighteen.'

'He's also getting divorced, has three children and is still half inclined to believe himself in love with you,' Caspar interjected.

'Saul was never in love with me,' Olivia refuted firmly. 'He may at one time have thought…felt… Oh, I'm sure Bobbie doesn't want to hear all this ancient family history,' she told her husband, then continued to explain to Bobbie, 'As a teenager I did have a bit of a crush on Saul, and then when his marriage broke up and Caspar and I were estranged, Saul provided a welcome cousinly shoulder for me to cry on. *His* wife was an American, by the way. In fact, it's rather ironic, given Gramps's insistence on being so anti-American, that two of us have married across the Atlantic, as it were.'

'If you ask me, a good deal of your grandfather's antipathy towards us springs from Ruth's mysterious relationship with her army major,' Caspar conjectured.

'Caspar, please,' Olivia objected even more sternly this time, and good manners precluded Bobbie from asking any questions. Instead, Olivia tactfully changed the subject and talked about how Haslewich had developed as a town. Her enthusiasm was infectious, but she admitted her knowledge was limited.

'If you really want to know more about its history, Ruth is the one to talk to. Which reminds me, I've got some books she loaned me and I really ought to get back to her. Could you possibly return them for me tomorrow, Bobbie, when you're out with Amelia?'

'Yes, of course,' Bobbie agreed.

'I'd take them back myself, after all she only lives a few minutes away from the office, but I'm in court in Chester tomorrow and possibly for the rest of the week, as well.'

'Oh and, Cas, before I forget, we've all been summoned to Queensmead for lunch on Sunday. Apparently, Max is home and Gramps has issued a royal summons. You're included, too,' she told Bobbie, adding ruefully, 'Not that it's likely to be a particularly relaxing occasion, not with Max around.'

'You'd have thought that marriage would have mellowed him a bit,' Caspar grumbled.

'The only thing that's ever likely to mellow Max is a large helping of humble pie,' Olivia responded forthrightly, 'and he's certainly not going to be fed that by Madeleine, who worships him.'

'Mmm…I've noticed,' Caspar agreed wryly. 'Hardly a healthy foundation on which to base a marriage and it can't but lead one to suspect that Max's motivation for marrying her—'

'Poor Madeleine,' Olivia broke in, 'I feel so sorry for her. She doesn't work and she's prepared to devote herself to Max and then to their children when they come along and, of course, she genuinely is a very lovable and kind-hearted person.

'And although Luke doesn't normally put in an appearance when he knows Max is going to be around, I suspect that we'll be seeing him at Queensmead *this* Sunday,' Olivia told Bobbie with a teasing smile.

Fortunately Amelia distracted them, freeing Bobbie from the necessity of making any reply, although she was uneasily aware that in refusing to correct Olivia's misconception that she and Luke were romantically involved, she was potentially risking tangling with an unstable situation, but, she told herself firmly, it was Luke's responsibility to tell his cousin exactly *why* he had virtually forced himself into her room, and not hers.

She was thinking about Luke again the following day as she wheeled Amelia through the sunshine and into Haslewich's pretty town square on her way to return Ruth's books. It was an unfathomable mystery to her how such a man—the type of man she would normally have sidestepped past with the same kind of politically correct disdain with which she would have avoided some offensively rabid right-winger spouting his views at a

Washington dinner party—could have such a deep and profound impact on her at the deepest level of her emotional and physical self, especially when there was so much else that was far more important to occupy her thoughts. It must be because she disliked him that she was spending so much time thinking about him, she decided hastily, but the analytical and fiercely sharp streak of hard-hitting perseverance and brutal self-honesty she had inherited via her father from his Puritan forebears refused to allow her such an easy way out. If she disliked him so much, how come he had the kind of physical effect on her body and her female desires that she couldn't remember having had so strongly or so bewilderingly activated since junior high?

So she was as vulnerable as the next woman to the kind of raw sexual energy that Luke positively exuded. So what? She knew otherwise perfectly sensible and intelligent women who went glassy-eyed over Brad Pitt and only admitted to it in the privacy of dark, sheltered wine bars after at least half a bottle of good wine.

Perhaps because she was thinking of Luke and therefore in defiance of her thoughts and his suspicions, she decided to wheel Amelia through the church walk instead of going straight across the square.

The walk ran along one side of the square and down to the gated church close that housed Ruth's home. All of the four benches were already filled, mainly with the town's more elderly residents, Bobbie noticed as she smiled in response to their admiring comments about Amelia. From the walk she could see the churchyard, and the temptation to visit it a second time proved irresistible. Amelia gurgled happily as she reached out to try to grab a handful of the pretty wild poppies that had seeded themselves in the grass verge and it was whilst Bobbie was gently detaching her from them that she heard someone calling her name.

Looking round she saw Ruth coming towards her. She was carrying an empty flower trug and explained, as she reached them, that she had been to do the church flowers.

'We were just on our way to see you,' Bobbie informed her quietly. 'Olivia asked me to return some books she borrowed from you and I thought that we'd take a small detour through the church walk,' she explained a little uncomfortably.

But to her relief Ruth didn't seem to share Luke's suspicious objections of her behaviour and simply replied, 'Yes, there's something fascinating about old churches. They always seem to hold such an air of peace and tranquillity. We can cut through here,' she added, indicating by waving her hand in the direction of the churchyard. 'It will save us walking all the way back.'

'It was here that I first met Joss,' Bobbie offered conversationally as they followed the path that meandered between the gravestones.

'Yes, I know,' Ruth returned. 'He often comes here. Jon and Jenny lost their first baby,' she explained quietly. 'He's buried here and Joss often comes to bring flowers and to talk to him. He's that kind of boy.'

'Yes, he is,' Bobbie agreed, suddenly discovering that there was a lump in her throat and that her eyes were filming with tears. Without really thinking about what she was saying, she murmured emotionally, 'That must just be the hardest thing…to lose a child…a baby.…'

There was a long silence before Ruth replied and when she did Bobbie could hear the tension in her voice as she responded, 'Yes, it is.… Here we are,' she said in a more normal voice, indicating a small gate set into the neatly clipped hedge that separated the churchyard from the close. 'We go this way.'

Ruth's home was everything that Bobbie had expected and a good many things she had not. The antique furniture, the Persian rugs, the smell of polish and flowers, the family heirlooms and photographs. She had known those would all be there, but the other things... A carefully chosen and displayed collection of polished stones and pebbles that were of no material value at all, other than the fact that someone—probably Joss—had found them and lovingly polished them to give to her; children's toys suitable for nephews and nieces of different ages; a book of modern flower arrangements and a rather racy novel along with several political biographies that Bobbie would never have thought of as typical reading for a spinster living in a quiet rural backwater.

On the bookshelves as well, though, were some very well-worn copies of Jane Austen's novels plus several leather-bound volumes of poetry.

Amelia, it was obvious, was delighted to be in the company of her great-great aunt and Bobbie was compelled to admire the very practised and confident way in which Ruth changed the baby's nappy, covering the little girl's face with kisses as she re-dressed her.

Angry with herself for her own emotional reaction, she had to turn her head away to hide tears as she watched the loving rapport between Amelia and Ruth. Bobbie, too, had great-great aunts but they were nothing like Ruth.

'It will be interesting to see if this young lady follows family tradition and chooses a career in law,' Ruth commented as she knelt back and looked from Amelia to Bobbie.

Bobbie took a deep breath. Here was her chance and she trembled in her shoes; Sam would not have sidestepped it and neither must she.

'Joss told me a little about the family's history. He said that the Haslewich branch was started by someone from Chester who broke away from his own family....'

'Yes,' Ruth agreed. 'Josiah was the youngest of three sons. He quarrelled with his father over his choice of a wife and was in effect disinherited. As a result he began his own practice here in Haslewich and, I suspect, because of the reason behind the split, there has always in the past been a distinct degree of rivalry between the two branches, more keenly felt in my observation by our branch than the family in Chester.' She gave Bobbie a friendly smile and asked, 'Do you have any brothers or sisters?'

Bobbie hesitated briefly before replying. 'I have a brother and a sister,' she said carefully, keeping her voice as neutral as she could before adding, 'As a matter of fact, my sister and I are twins. She's called Samantha.'

'Twins…' Ruth raised her eyebrows. 'What a coincidence. Of course you know by now, that twins feature very heavily in our genealogy and in fact…'

Bobbie's heart was thumping just a little bit too heavily as she listened to Ruth talk about the occurrence of twins in the Crighton family. But she was also obviously interested in finding out more about Bobbie's parents.

'Olivia mentioned that your father was a politician…?'

'Yes, he is,' Bobbie confirmed and felt pressured to add as Ruth waited patiently, 'My father's family are from New England—that's where Sam and I grew up. But he and my mother spend a lot of time in Washington.'

'Does your mother have a career?'

'No…not now.' Bobbie bit her lip as she heard the curtness in her own voice. 'She…we… My mother hasn't been very well lately,' she said quietly. 'And we…my…my father… No, she doesn't have a career.'

Ruth eyed her young guest thoughtfully, sensing not just Bobbie's reluctance to talk about her family and in particular her mother, but also her unexpressed concern and anguish over her mother's health, remembering how she had felt when she had lost her own mother, her only support in a household that was ruled by her father and his prejudices—prejudices that to a great extent had been backed up and continued by her brother.

'You're obviously very concerned about your mother,' she said with gentle sympathy. 'If you're worried about using Olivia's telephone to ring home, I'm sure if you explained the situation to her, she'd be only too glad for you to do so. If she isn't, which I can't imagine, then you must certainly feel free to come over here and telephone from here.' When Bobbie stared at her, she added quietly, 'I do know what it's like to be separated from someone you love, you know. How it feels to worry about them, to imagine all manner of horrid things happening to them when you aren't there to help, to be with them.'

'My mother had a serious operation last year and she still hasn't fully recovered.' Bobbie swallowed back the tears she could feel thickening at the back of her throat. What on earth had come over her?

The nature of her mother's illness—the change in her from a positive, warm, happy person to someone who could, at times, be so desperately low—had shocked and frightened them all. It was regarded as a family secret they had all instinctively and automatically chosen to keep closely hidden in order to protect not just their mother, but their father, as well. Normally Bobbie would no more have dreamt of discussing her mother's health with someone outside their immediate family than she would have taken off her clothes and walked naked through the streets of her home town. And now, feeling that she had not just broken some sacred rule but also, and even more distressingly, betrayed her mother into the bargain, she found it hard to both understand why she had mentioned her mother's health at all and to forgive herself for having done so.

'I must go,' she told Ruth, standing up and picking Amelia up as she did so. 'Caspar will be back soon and he'll wonder where we are.'

'I expect I shall see you on Sunday,' Ruth said as she escorted her to the door, and then, to Bobbie's shock, as she turned to leave, Ruth reached out and touched her arm lightly. 'Try not to let your very natural concern for your mother make you over-fearful. I'm sure if there was anything you should know that your sister would tell you. It's easy enough for me to say, I realise,' she added ruefully, 'but I was once your age and I do know how it feels to…to worry about someone you love.…'

As she spoke she looked down at Amelia and said inconsequentially, 'Babies always seem so very vulnerable.…'

'Perhaps because they are,' Bobbie returned curtly. 'After all, they have no control over how they're treated, have they? They're totally dependent on the adults around them for everything. Protection…nourishment…love!'

Bobbie's head was aching by the time she had returned to Olivia and Caspar's. Tonight was one of her evenings off and she intended to drive into Chester, ostensibly to call at the Grosvenor to check if there were any messages for her but, in reality, in order to telephone her sister.

At the Grosvenor the receptionist remembered her and greeted her with a warm smile. There were no messages but Bobbie hadn't expected any, and fortunately the lobby was relatively empty as she went to use the pay phone.

Samantha answered her call so quickly that Bobbie guessed she had been waiting impatiently for her to ring.

After giving her the pay phone number, Bobbie waited for her to call back, glancing around the foyer as she did so and then freezing as she spotted Luke on the opposite side of the room, standing by the entrance to the restaurant. Fortunately he had not seen her, and as the telephone rang, Bobbie turned her back on him and made herself as inconspicuous as possible, praying that he would not do so. He had been talking to another man, and Bobbie kept her fingers crossed that the pair of them were on the way to have dinner in the restaurant.

On hearing about the family gathering on Sunday, Samantha excitedly said that that would be the perfect time for Bobbie to stand up and say what they had rehearsed. She was quite adamant that the time for retribution had arrived.

'I know,' Bobbie agreed steadily, 'but—'

'But me no buts,' Samantha insisted fiercely and then, relenting, Bobbie heard her twin saying in a softer voice, 'Love you, Bo bo....'

Bo bo had been her childhood nickname and Bobbie felt her eyes filling and was torn between laughter and tears as she heard Sam use it now.

'Love you, too, Sam,' she returned shakily, her voice husky with emotion as she blew a kiss into the receiver before replacing it and then murmuring, 'Oh, Sam, I miss you,' before she started to turn round.

Bobbie stiffened apprehensively as she heard Luke saying cynically over his shoulder, 'Joss, Max and now *Sam*... You certainly like to share your favours around generously, don't you?'

Unable to believe her ears, Bobbie shot back furiously, 'For your information, Sam is...Sam is very, very special to me.'

'Really.' Luke's eyes narrowed as he told her grittily, 'You do surprise me. From the way you responded to me, it didn't feel like there was anyone even special in your life, never mind *very, very* special.'

Bobbie could feel her face growing hot as she hissed back at him before turning on her heel and heading determinedly for the exit, 'I did not respond to you. You made a grab for me.'

She pushed through the door and walked out onto the street, thankful to feel the cool night air on her burning face and even more thankful to have left Luke and his barbed comments behind her in the hotel foyer. Only, as she quickly discovered, she hadn't left him behind after all. Angrily she glared at him before she demanded, 'Go away. Stop following me.'

'I am not following you,' Luke contradicted her forcefully, 'and neither did I make a "grab" for you as you term it.'

'Oh yes, you did,' Bobbie argued back insistently, the heat returning to her face as she realised that they were attracting the amused looks of people entering the hotel. Quickly she instinctively sought the protective cover of a nearby shadowy gap between the buildings. 'You made a grab for me and you…you assaulted me,' Bobbie accused Luke furiously as he followed her into the shadows, ignoring the inner voice that warned her that the language she was using was dangerously close to being deliberately aggressive as well as not totally true.

'Assaulted you…? I did no such thing,' Luke denied grimly. 'I kissed you, yes, but if the reaction you gave me was anything to go by…'

'That was a fluke…a mistake—I was thinking of someone else,' Bobbie defended herself quickly. 'It could never happen again.'

'No?' Luke challenged her softly.

'No,' Bobbie answered, but she knew her voice lacked conviction and she looked apprehensively past Luke, desperate to escape from him and the situation she herself had helped to create, before any further damage was done either to her ego or her credibility. 'Look, I've got to go,' she informed him. 'The last bus for Haslewich leaves at ten and—'

'The last *bus.*'

Bobbie could see that he was frowning.

'Surely Olivia offered you the use of a car…?'

'Yes, she did,' Bobbie agreed steadily, 'but since I was coming into Chester on my own personal business and Olivia had to use the car this evening, I felt it was unfair of me to borrow it.'

'Then you're a fool,' Luke scolded her roundly. 'No woman should take the risk of having to wait for, or travel, on public transport on her own late at night these days unless she has to. I'll drive you home.'

Bobbie tried to protest but he refused to accept her claim that she was perfectly safe, telling her chillingly instead that he had seen far too many assault cases where the victim had been a young woman travelling on her own to take the risk of her swelling their numbers.

'I'm over six foot and hardly vulnerable,' Bobbie felt bound to point out.

'You're a woman,' Luke told her flatly, 'and as for not being vulnerable…height has nothing to do with it. Although, I suppose from your point of view, it's only natural that you should feel defensive about it. For a woman to be so unusually tall must be—'

'Must be what?' Bobbie demanded furiously. 'Must be a turn-off to men? Well, *you* might find it one, but I can promise you…'

They were out in the square now, Luke having taken hold of her arm whilst they were arguing and cleverly outmanoeuvred her almost without her realising what he was doing.

'I'm parked over here,' he told her without letting go of her and then adding in the same, almost casual, tone,

'I have no idea what it was you were about to promise me, but what *I* can promise *you* is that personally, while any woman with hang-ups about her body can be something of a turn-off, the thought of having to contort myself into a position suitable for making love with a woman more than several inches shorter than I am myself is even more of one and, in fact, there is something that is very much a turn-on being physically matched with a woman who fits neatly into my own body.'

Bobbie could feel her face starting to burn even more hotly with a mixture of chagrin and a shocking sense of sensual excitement whose existence felt like it was choking her. 'Joss told me you liked petite dumb blondes,' she countered weakly.

'Joss has made the same mistake that too many other people make,' Luke informed her dryly. 'It's the petite dumb blondes who prefer *me*, not the other way round.'

They had reached his car now, a large, roomy BMW, Bobbie was relieved to see. Olivia's car, nippy though it was, had her hunching over the steering wheel, her back aching after she had driven it for any great distance.

As he stood next to her, deactivating the alarm and preparing to open the passenger door for her, she heard Luke saying softly, 'I'm a lawyer by training and by custom and it would be illogical of me to prefer a sexual partner with whom even the mildest form of sensual pleasure would be physically ungratifying.'

When he saw the way Bobbie was frowning back at him in confusion, Luke closed the distance between them and, putting his hands on her waist, drew her firmly against his body so that they were standing thigh to thigh, torso to torso.

Bobbie took a deep, protesting breath, about to launch herself into a furious verbal attack and then stopped as the very act of drawing breath brought her into sharp awareness of exactly what Luke meant.

'See what I mean,' he whispered as the grip of his hands tightened. 'If I were to kiss you now, it wouldn't just be our mouths that made matching and sensual physical contact, would it?'

As she felt herself starting to tremble, Bobbie wasn't sure if her reaction was caused by anger or...or what? Not physical awareness of Luke, surely...not physical arousal, physical responsiveness to him.

'If this is some kind of joke...' she began warily as she tried to step back from him.

'It's no joke,' Luke responded grimly. 'No joke at all,' he repeated in a much softer tone as he bent his head towards her and his hands started to slide caressingly down over the curves of her behind, pulling her even more intimately into his own body so that... Bobbie held her breath, the sensation of Luke's body against her own somehow activating a dangerous physical transformation within her and an even more dangerous reaction without. She had experienced physical arousal before, physical attraction, and she knew perfectly well just how illusionary and charismatic it could be—and how meaninglessly empty—but this sensation, this feeling...this emotion that held her in such shocking and powerful thrall, was far too intense and overwhelming to be that. It was more, much more, than the provocative thrust of Luke's body against hers and the fierce primal throb of desire quickening within her own, more than the sexually charged atmosphere of heat and need she could feel shimmering around them. So strong that she could almost reach out and touch it, taste it...just as she felt she wanted to reach out and touch and taste Luke himself.

All of those feelings, no matter how strong, how shocking, how unwanted they were to her, were capable of analysis and explanation; a cause for them could be found and once found they themselves could be dismissed. But there was no cause, no means of analysing or understanding, never mind denying or dismissing that shock wave of emotional oneness and rightness she had experienced as Luke drew her close to him; that bewildering notion that somehow she had found that special wondrous place; that special wondrous person who was her real home, that knowledge that somehow or other Luke had reached out and touched the very core of her innermost being and that because of that…because of *him* the whole of her life would be changed for ever.

Bobbie had always assumed that one day she would fall in love deeply and permanently and she had hoped that when she did that love would be returned; that together she and her beloved would form a close-knit unit that would one day expand to include the children she hoped they would have, but it had never occurred to her that loving could ever be like this; that from one moment to the next, one heartbeat to the next, she would suddenly and irrevocably know the man she loved and know just as intensely her love for him could never be destroyed.

'Luke…' As she said his name on a shakily expelled breath, he covered her mouth with his, his hands coming up to cup her face and hold her still beneath his kiss. His thumb caressed the delicate curve of her cheek as his mouth moved equally caressingly on hers.

To Bobbie it seemed the most natural thing in the world to respond openly to him, reaching out to hold him, opening her mouth to him and welcoming the demanding thrust of his tongue within it with a soft, throaty murmur of delight.

Even their mouths might have been made to fit together, she acknowledged hazily as she purred her pleasure into his caressing mouth, arching her throat beneath the stroking touch of his hand, feeling her pulse quicken and her body tense as her nipples tightened beneath her clothes and the urge to press herself even closer to him became too strong to resist.

'Luke…' As he started to lift his mouth from hers, she whispered his name protestingly, reluctantly opening her eyes, their pupils dilated with passion, her expression softly drugged with all that she was feeling as she caught hold of his arm, intending to guide the hand he had let fall from her throat to her breast. And then, abruptly, she realised what she was doing and with whom, and like someone coming out of a trance her body stiffened as she cried out fiercely, 'No!'

'No,' Luke agreed tersely as he, too, stepped back. He looked almost as shocked as she felt herself, Bobbie recognised, but that was impossible. There was no way *he* could be feeling the same emotional turmoil she was experiencing; the same anguished jolt of recognition and yearning so strong that it left her feeling physically dazed and weak, coupled with fear and panic and the self-protective need to blot out and deny the existence of such feelings to remind herself that he was, at best, a man she should treat with circumspection and caution and, at worst, someone who could turn out to be her most powerful foe.

And yes, she had quite definitely mistaken that look of shock she had thought she had seen in his eyes, she acknowledged achingly now as she looked at him and saw the hardness of his compressed mouth and the cold way he was watching her.

'You shouldn't have done that,' she told him shakily.

'Why?' he asked derisively. 'Because Sam, whoever he is, wouldn't like it?'

For a moment Bobbie simply looked at him and then said quietly before she started to turn around to walk away from him, 'Sam is not a *he*, she's a *she*, and she's also my sister, my *twin* sister,' she emphasised.

'Where do you think you're going?' he challenged her as he deliberately blocked her way.

'To catch a bus,' she replied simply.

'I've already told you, I'll drive you home.'

Bobbie toyed briefly with the idea of not just defying him but also of actively pushing her way past him, but as her eyes met his she read a warning in them that she would be very foolish to try to do so. It was a rather odd sensation to be aware of being so femininely vulnerable and powerless as she had lost count of the number of men over the years who had made jokey and not-so-jokey remarks to her about not wanting to get on her bad side, hinting that because of her height she was somehow less emotionally a woman than her shorter sisters.

In a face to face confrontation with Luke, she was all too likely to come off the loser, she recognised, and he certainly had no inhibitions at all about getting on her wrong side. Silently she turned round and walked back to the car.

'So Sam is your twin sister,' Luke commented once they were both in the car and he had driven out of the car park. 'Have you any other family?'

'Why the sudden interest in my family?' Bobbie asked him.

'Perhaps because I'm curious to know the reason for *your* interest in mine,' Luke returned silkily.

Bobbie bit her lip. She had walked straight into that one.

'I have a brother. My parents are both alive and so is my grandfather on my mother's side. And although both my parents were only children, their parents came from large families, so we have any number of great-aunts and uncles as well as a whole string of second and third cousins.'

'Twins are normally very close,' Luke commented. 'Are you and your sister?'

'Yes,' Bobbie affirmed curtly.

'You must miss her.'

'Yes. I do.'

'Presumably she couldn't come with you?'

'No, she couldn't,' Bobbie responded in a tone of voice that indicated she didn't want to answer any more questions, but Luke refused to take the hint.

'Why was that?' he pressed.

'She had other commitments,' Bobbie told him repressively, turning her head to look out of the window into the darkness as an added signal that she didn't want him to keep interrogating her. So far as she was concerned, her sister was not a subject she wanted to discuss with him.

'Other commitments. What does that mean? Is she married...does she have a family?'

'No, she is not married and she does not have a family. If you must know, she is part way through her master's and couldn't take time off and that was why...'

Bobbie stopped.

'That was why what?' Luke asked suavely.

'That was why I had to come on my own,' Bobbie answered shakily, disturbed by how easily she had almost betrayed herself.

'Had to,' Luke repeated incisively. 'Surely your trip could have been postponed until after her college work was finished or fitted in during her vacations.'

'Maybe it could,' Bobbie agreed, 'but I wanted to come to Europe.'

'Without your sister, your twin, even though you've just told me how close you are and how much you miss her? What exactly *are* you doing here in Haslewich, Bobbie, and why all the interest in my family?'

Bobbie drew in a sharp breath. 'What is it exactly

you're trying to imply?' she demanded. 'I'm here in Haslewich because I'm working for Olivia, and as for my interest in your family…' She paused.

'Yes,' Luke encouraged grimly.

'I was just interested, that's all,' Bobbie fibbed weakly, giving a small shrug. 'It's not against the law, is it?'

To her relief they were almost in Haslewich; another ten minutes or so and she would safely be back at Olivia's.

'That all depends, doesn't it,' Luke answered as he turned into the road that led to the house, 'on what it is you're really doing here. I *know* you're lying to me, Bobbie,' he told her as he brought the car to a stop on the drive and turned to look at her. 'What I *don't* know as yet is *why* you're lying and what it is you're trying to conceal…what it is you're really doing here, but I promise you that I intend to find out…'

Bobbie climbed out of the car and shut the door firmly.

'Wasn't that Luke's car?' Olivia asked as she let Bobbie in.

'Yes, I bumped into him in Chester and he brought me home,' Bobbie told her.

'Oh, why didn't he come in?' As she looked into Bobbie's face, she asked gently, 'Oh dear, you two haven't had a fight, have you?'

To her own consternation, Bobbie suffered the indignity of feeling her eyes start to fill with tears. If there was one ultimate folly in a woman of six foot plus, it was surely crying in public.

'Oh, Bobbie, don't worry,' Olivia soothed her as she gave her a quick, firm hug. 'I'm *sure* the two of you will soon make it up.'

'I don't want to make it up,' Bobbie declared defiantly, sniffing. 'I hate him.'

'Oh dear,' Olivia commiserated. 'That bad, was it?'

'That's right, take it out on the weeds,' Bobbie heard Ruth's amused voice telling her the next day as she tugged viciously at the weeds in Olivia's herbaceous border whilst Amelia slept peacefully in her stroller nearby.

Hot and grubby, her face flushed and her hair tousled, Bobbie hadn't heard Ruth arrive and now she turned round, her mouth forming a startled 'Oh' of surprise.

'I used to do very much the same thing when my father or brother were being particularly chauvinistic and difficult,' Ruth confided to Bobbie as she walked across the grass towards her, 'and I'm afraid I even used to give vent to the most undaughterly and unsisterly feelings beneath my breath, which was a most unacceptable thing for one to do in those days.'

When she saw the way Bobbie was looking at her, she explained gently, 'You see, I grew up in an era where one was obliged to accept that one did what one's parents, especially one's father, thought best. His word was law. My mother was very much the old-fashioned type of wife and my father rather stern and autocratic, very decided in his views and opinions.'

Her face clouded a little. 'In many ways our lives were over-restricted and limited, the brief taste of freedom we were given during the war when we were needed all too swiftly snatched away again once our usefulness was over, and yet I suspect there was a certain security in knowing what was expected of us.

'Luke, I know, can seem rather autocratic and severe at times. Like all of us, Luke, too, has suffered from being a victim of this family's overriding need to prove themselves worthy of being a Crighton. It's a handicap that has been passed down from generation to generation, from father to son, as the virtues and achievements of past Crightons are extolled from babyhood almost and the growing child informed that it is his duty to prove himself worthy of following in the same footsteps.

'Fortunately things are changing. Jon's children, while they all are determined to take up the law as a career, are also resilient and have a sense of independence, of self-worth, a belief in themselves, which hopefully will free them from the expectations that controlled earlier generations' lives. Apart from Max, who unfortunately is cast in a very different mold... Perhaps marriage to Madeleine will change him. I hope so for her sake.'

'Why are you telling me all this?' Bobbie asked her uncertainly.

'Why?' Ruth tilted her head on one side and studied Bobbie for a moment. 'Perhaps because I like you and I hate to see you looking so unhappy. Luke may not be perfect but I do believe that the handicaps that come with being a Crighton could be very much alleviated in him, given the right encouragement. It isn't always easy to say why we should be so instantly drawn to one person and not to another,' Ruth added gently.

'In fact, for most of us, it's very hard to accept, never mind admit, that we have such feelings, that we're capable of such instant and illogical, emotional reactions. Why I should be so specifically drawn to you, Bobbie, I can't say. All I *can* say is that I am, in much the same way that out of all my great-nieces and nephews, Joss and this young lady here have a special place in my heart. It doesn't mean that I love the others any the less, merely that I love these two just that little bit more. How is your mother by the way?'

Bobbie's hand jerked as she lost her grip on the weed she had been trying to work loose, glad that Ruth couldn't see her face as she replied in a choked voice,

'I…she's still not very well. Her…her doctor has suggested that she should consider going into analysis,' Bobbie elaborated reluctantly.

'It isn't analysis Mom needs,' Samantha had denied passionately when she had been telling Bobbie this latest piece of family news. 'It's—'

'I know what it is, Sam,' she had responded, 'but we can't give it to her. No one can.'

'Maybe not, but at least we can have the satisfaction of knowing they haven't got away with what they've done, that they're being punished, too.'

'Two wrongs don't make a right, Sam,' Bobbie had remonstrated gently to her sister, but Sam, as she had known she would, had refused to accept such a point of view.

Sam would never have got herself in the situation she had managed to get herself in, Bobbie acknowledged. She knew that Sam was expecting her to make use of the family gathering on Sunday to reveal her true identity, to speak out and make the denouncement they had planned, to shame the person responsible for her mother's unhappiness by publicly revealing what they had done.

'Amelia's waking up,' she told Ruth unnecessarily as they both heard the little girl start to gurgle. 'I'd better take her in and get cleaned up. It's almost time for her lunch.'

Ruth wasn't Bobbie's only unexpected visitor that day. Joss arrived later in the afternoon looking both pleased with himself and slightly self-conscious as he hugged the baby and then proceeded to tell Bobbie about the family of otters he had seen playing in the river as he cycled past.

'Mum says that you're going to Gramps's on Sunday,' he remarked.

'Yes, that's right,' Bobbie agreed neutrally.

'You mustn't mind if Gramps says anything to you about your being American,' Joss told her earnestly. 'He doesn't mean... Well, he's not... Mum says that a lot of his grumpiness is because of the pain in his hip.'

Bobbie tried to stop her mouth from twitching in wry amusement at Joss's unguarded honesty.

He stayed for almost an hour drinking Bobbie's home-made lemonade and eating the cookies she had baked earlier in the afternoon for Caspar, who had teased Olivia that at last he had found someone who could make him proper American cookies.

'Do you know something, Bobbie?' Joss confided to her as he got up to leave. 'You really look like one of my cousins, only she's got red hair—that's Meg, Saul's daughter. She's only four, though, but Aunt Ruth noticed it, as well,' he added informatively.

Bobbie was glad there was no one there but Joss to witness the shock his words had caused her and fortunately he was too engrossed in finishing off his last cookie to look directly at her. If he had...

Bobbie could remember Saul from the party. Tall, dark-haired, good-looking and very sexy. He had once been in love with Olivia, Caspar had told her. He was now in his mid-thirties, over a decade younger than her mother. How ironic that Joss should comment that while she and Saul's child looked alike, *she* had red hair.

'See you on Sunday,' Joss called out to her as he rode off.

Oh yes, she would definitely see him, but Bobbie doubted that he would ever look so warmly on her again.

It had all seemed so simple when she and Sam had discussed it at home. So easy. So straightforward and right. Then she had expected that the hardest thing she would have to do would be to get close enough to the family to put their plan into action.

'It's no good just going for a one-to-one confrontation,' Samantha had insisted when Bobbie had suggested this course.

'Perhaps if I just explained how Mom feels, how it has affected her, how much she needs to know *why* she was so ruthlessly rejected.'

'That won't work,' Samantha had told her. 'There's no point in appealing to someone's finer feelings or their sense of compassion when it's obvious that they don't have any. No! What we have to do is to show them up for what they are, confront them in public in front of their family.'

It had never occurred to her then that once she actually met the family she would like them. Well, certain members of it at least, she amended hastily, dismissing the far too detailed and accurate mental portrait of Luke her memory had just supplied her with. People who had just been names to her at first were now so very much more.

What did a person do when the facts led in one direction and one's emotions in another that was completely opposite? How did one make a decision—a judgement—like the one *she* had to make? She wasn't used to playing God and it wasn't a role that sat easily on her shoulders, but then...

'Think of Mom...think of what she's suffered...how she's been hurt,' Samantha had urged her, and Bobbie only had to picture her mother's face when she talked about her past to be filled with the same aching, angry, but helpless feeling of furious resentment on her behalf that she had experienced when she had first heard what had happened.

'We can't alter what's been done,' her father had said gently once to Bobbie when, as a teenager, she had burst into an impassioned speech about the unhappiness in her mother's past.

'But it's all so unfair,' Bobbie had protested. 'It nearly even stopped you and Mom getting married.'

'I know. I know,' her father agreed. 'But fortunately your grandfather was able to make it a bit easier for us. He used that special brand of Southern charm he has to coax the family around.' Her father chuckled. 'It was certainly the first time I've ever seen Great-Aunt Emma actually flirting.'

'Great-Aunt Emma flirted with Grandpa...?' She stood wide-eyed.

'She certainly did, and then, of course, when they realised that he was connected through his mother's side to an influential and wealthy family...'

'They still didn't really want you to marry Mom, though, did they, Dad, even though Grandpa is very rich and Mom his only child...?'

'No, they didn't,' her father affirmed honestly. 'But I can tell you this, when you love someone as much as I love your mother, no power on earth can stop you from being together. The reason I wanted my family to accept and value her was because I knew it was what *she* wanted. As far as I was concerned, I'd have gladly turned my back on the whole pack of them rather than lose your mother.'

'Even your parents?' Bobbie asked him quietly.

'Even my folks,' her father agreed. 'Don't misunderstand me, Bobbie. I loved them very much and I had a great deal of respect for them. I still do. But I love your mom more...much, much more. You see, honey, the kind of love you have for that one special person in your life is just so different from any other kind of love that once you've experienced it... Well, you just wait and see.'

'I wouldn't want to fall in love with someone you and Mom didn't like,' Bobbie had protested.

Prophetic words. She could just imagine how her parents, especially her mother, would feel if she were to announce that she had fallen in love with a Crighton. Fallen in love with? Bobbie tensed.

Restlessly she paced the room. She *wasn't* in love with Luke....

She wasn't silly enough to let herself fall in love with someone like Luke. She had far too much regard for her own emotional well-being, too strong a sense of self-esteem, too much awareness of the pain that lay ahead of her in loving a man who not only most assuredly did not return her feelings but who, even if he *had*, was quite simply someone she could never share her life with.

Yet, perversely, instead of looking forward to Sunday in the knowledge that once it was over, once she had carried out the task that had originally brought her to Cheshire, she would be free to leave and return home, safe from any more heart-searching over Luke who surely, with the Atlantic safely between them, would quickly become nothing more than a distant—a very distant—memory, Bobbie acknowledged that she was actually dreading it.

But of course, there was nothing that she could do to stop Sunday coming. Nothing at all!

CHAPTER SIX

QUEENSMEAD was very much as she had pictured it, Bobbie realised: a large, gracious house set in its own grounds reached via a traditional sweeping drive, its seventeenth-century stone façade draped in the soft tendrils of a huge wisteria.

Although ostensibly Bobbie was merely attending the family get-together as Amelia's temporary nanny, virtually as soon as they had entered the house, Olivia had deftly removed Amelia from her arms and told Bobbie firmly that she was to make sure she enjoyed herself and that *she* was certainly going to enjoy showing her daughter off to her relatives.

Despite its generous proportions, the large drawing room was very crowded. Jon and Jenny, who had arrived ahead of them with the twins, Joss and Olivia's younger brother, claimed her attention whilst Louise and Katie thanked her for the small antique brooches she had given them as their eighteenth-birthday presents.

'I'll have to take you over to introduce you to Gramps,' Olivia told her as she handed Amelia over to an admiring Jenny.

'Ben's not in a very good mood, I'm afraid,' Jenny warned them ruefully, adding quietly, 'I think having Max here reminds him of your father, Olivia. I rather think he feels that Jon isn't doing as much as he could to try to track David down.'

'Dad won't be found unless he wants to be found,' Olivia responded tersely. 'I just wish that Gramps could see that, but then he's always had a blind spot where

Dad is concerned. I wish sometimes I could tell him the truth,' she declared fiercely.

'I doubt that he would believe you if you did. He needs to cling on to his faith in David, his belief in him,' Jenny told her wisely. 'I'm sorry, Bobbie,' Jenny apologised. 'We're being very rude, talking about family matters and ignoring you.'

'Bobbie *is* almost a member of the family,' Olivia insisted and then added slyly, 'and very soon she might become one officially, as well.'

Whilst Bobbie protested, her cheeks burning hotly, Jenny gave her an interested look but didn't press the matter, leaving it to Olivia to explain.

'Luke's pretty smitten with Bobbie,' she elaborated whilst teasingly shaking her head as Bobbie tried to contradict what she was saying. 'It's no good,' Olivia said, laughing. 'The pair of you have given yourselves away too clearly to start denying it now.'

'Hello there. I was hoping we might get to meet again.'

Bobbie turned thankfully towards Max as he strolled over to join them, his arrival a welcome interruption, although it was obvious that Olivia didn't think so because almost immediately she announced, 'I was just about to take Bobbie to introduce her to Gramps, Max, so I'm afraid you'll have to excuse us.'

'You haven't met my grandfather yet?' Max asked Bobbie, pointedly ignoring his cousin as he turned his back to her, effectively blocking her out of the conversation. Instead, he concentrated on Bobbie, giving her the benefit of his heated crocodile smile and a look that slid slowly from the top of her head all the way down to her toes. It lingered appreciatively on her body in a manner that was both extremely practised and, so far as Bobbie was concerned, extremely unappealing, but she kept her thoughts to herself, waiting politely whilst Max reached out and tucked her hand through his arm as he told her, 'Come with me, but let me warn you that he—'

'Doesn't like Americans,' Bobbie supplied dryly for him. 'Yes, so I've been told.'

'It isn't an aversion I share,' Max assured her softly with another appreciative look. 'Far from it.'

'But your wife, I believe, is British,' Bobbie pointed out sweetly, just ever so slightly emphasising the words 'your wife'.

'Very much so,' Max agreed suavely, looking more amused than concerned that she should have reminded him that he was a married man, confirming her inward assessment of him when he continued, 'My wife is also small, plump and, I'm afraid, rather plain and a brunette, while I, I must admit, have a penchant for long-legged blondes, especially when they're as beautiful as you are.'

His audacity was unbelievable, Bobbie decided as she replied with cool firmness, 'Really. Unfortunately *I* do not have a penchant for married men, especially those as unkind about the woman they've chosen to marry as you have just been. Please excuse me,' she added as she detached herself from him and started to move away.

Only she didn't get very far because as she turned round, to her consternation, she found her way blocked by Luke. When had he arrived and why was he looking at her like that?

'Er…Luke,' she faltered as guiltily as a child caught with her fingers in the cookie jar, as she later angrily told herself.

'Luke,' she heard Max drawling in a far more composed voice, 'I was just taking Bobbie over to introduce her to Grandfather.'

'Really. Via a rather long detour I can only presume,' Luke returned coldly as Max looked innocently round the empty room he had brought her to and told him, 'Your grandfather is in the library with your wife.'

'Oh, is he? That's obviously why we couldn't find him, then,' Max replied cheerfully, but he made no attempt to remain with them, Bobbie noticed, excusing himself with some vague comment about needing to speak with his father and leaving Bobbie on her own to face Luke's obvious ire.

'I might have known,' Luke said grimly. 'I imagine it must be a case of like to like, but let me warn you, if you're hoping to get anything more than a very brief tumble in bed and the dubious pleasure of boosting Max's ego out of him, you're going to be very disappointed.'

'There's obviously not much to choose between you, then, is there?' Bobbie quipped, using flippancy to cover the churning havoc his presence was creating in her body.

She knew she had gone too far, though, when Luke turned towards her, reaching for her wrists, his teeth baring in a feral smile of high-octane anger, but before he could say or do anything, mercifully Olivia popped her head round the door.

'Not *still* quarrelling? I thought you'd have made it up by now, the pair of you. You should be kissing and making up, not fighting....'

She was gone before either one could say anything, responding to Caspar's summons from the other side of the door, leaving Luke to demand savagely, 'And just what the hell was that all about?'

'Olivia thinks that you and I...that we're...that we're romantically involved,' Bobbie informed him shakily.

'She what?'

'Don't blame *me*. *I'm* not the one who dragged *you* into my hotel room and then left a note at the reception desk that anyone could have seen,' Bobbie reminded him grittily. 'You were keen enough to have *Fenella* think we were involved. It's a pity that you didn't think a little harder and realise that others might make the same mistake.'

'I see, and you, of course, being the person you are, obviously haven't thought it desirable to put Olivia right.'

The sarcastic contempt dripping from his words made Bobbie flinch, but she was determined not to let him see just how much he was hurting her.

'Why should *I* do your dirty work for you?' she challenged him spiritedly.

'Why indeed,' he returned unpleasantly, 'especially when you could have some hidden agenda of your own that makes it an advantage for you to be publicly, at least, romantically attached to me?'

He had come perilously close, too close, to guessing the truth for Bobbie's peace of mind, guilt and anxiety panicking her into reacting angrily. 'There couldn't be *any* advantage, *public* or *private*, that would make me want that—or you,' she denied vehemently.

'No!' Luke contradicted her firmly. 'That isn't the way *I* remember certain events—far from it. In fact, while I hate to call you a liar,' he drawled unkindly, 'there have been at least two occasions *I* can call to mind when *you* evinced anything but reluctance to demonstrate just the opposite.'

Bobbie glared at him. 'If you're referring to the way you forced yourself on me…the way you kissed me totally against my will…' She stopped, her face flushing as she saw the way Luke was looking at her. 'I…I've told you before,' she started to protest defensively. 'I was thinking about someone else.'

Wildly she started to head for the half-open door, knowing that she was on unsafe ground, very unsafe ground indeed, but she was still unable to resist one final act of defiance in the face of his accusations.

'Under normal circumstances,' she raged furiously,

'there's just no way I'd respond to you and anyway I *wasn't* responding to *you*...I was...' She shook her head. What was the point in arguing with him? The sensible thing to do would be quite simply to walk away from him right now.

But unfortunately she had left it a little too late. Luke's gaze was already mercilessly fixed on her and as she measured the distance between them and the narrow doorway he was blocking, he sprang into action, catching hold of her as she tried to run past him and imprisoning her easily in his arms despite her attempts to struggle free. Kicking the door shut and enclosing them both in the semi-darkness of the room, he pushed her back against the closed door.

'You're sure about that, are you?' he demanded mockingly.

'Of course I'm sure,' Bobbie lied through gritted teeth. 'And even if I wasn't, I don't get *any* kicks from...from physical violence,' she told him bitingly.

She could feel Luke's anger as he absorbed the impact of her angry remark, and her own body tensed in wary response. How much, after all, did she actually know about him? How much did she...?

'Neither do I,' she heard him telling her curtly and with so much distaste in his voice that she knew he was speaking the truth. 'But I don't like liars,' he continued. 'When I kissed you, *you* responded to *me*.'

'*I* responded to being *kissed*,' Bobbie protested. 'It had *nothing* to do with you. You were...I thought you were someone else,' she lied again.

'Is that a fact? Well, let's just put that to the test, shall we?' Luke told her and she could tell from the deceptive softness of his voice that he was very, very angry, indeed, far more angry in fact, than he had been when he had physically stopped her from leaving.

The panic that flared inside her and had her struggling

and trying to break free from his imprisoning grip had nothing to do with any fear or horror at the thought of being kissed or even touched by him. No, it was the fear, her fear, of what she might do, how she might react when he did that was urging her to struggle so desperately to break free of him, Bobbie acknowledged. But all her struggles could not break his firm hold of her. All they were doing, she had to admit, was exhausting her strength and bruising her ego far worse than his strong hands on her wrists were likely to be bruising her flesh.

He waited until she paused to draw a deep lungful of air before releasing her wrists so that he could use his arms to bind her tightly against him, so tightly that she could feel the hard imprint of his body against her own, even through both their layers of clothing, Bobbie realised. So closely that...

'Look at me, Bobbie,' she heard him commanding her grimly, and to her own self-disgust she found that she was obeying him, lifting her gaze to meet his. 'Good,' he told her mock-softly. 'Now we both know that this time you know exactly who I am, don't we?' And before she could argue or object, he did what she had known he intended to do all along and what she had told herself she would resist with every ounce of her mental, emotional and physical strength. He bent his head and started to kiss her.

It was a bruising, hard, angry kiss that cerebrally Bobbie realised should have left her completely cold and unmoved, a kiss of icy, arrogant male passion, born of a male need to dominate and conquer, the kind of kiss a conquering warlord would give a captive victim and yet, the moment his mouth touched hers, Bobbie knew she was lost.

Oh, she still felt angry—bitterly, furiously so—still resented what he was doing, resented him. She still re-

jected with her mind, her reason, everything he was,
everything he was doing to her, but her body, her senses,
had urges and needs of their own and to them the hard
possession of Luke's kiss had nothing of the gloating
male triumph her mind flinched from, none of the sense
of subjugation that her feminine pride fought so hard
against. No, they saw and felt only a heady sense of
power and heat; a sweet, soaring obliterating surge of
feminine triumph that she…they, could make this man,
who resented her so much, who disliked her so much,
ache so much for her that he couldn't stop himself from
touching her, kissing her, wanting her and most empow-
ering of all, reacting to her. And wantonly they played
on that reaction, teasing it, enticing it, inciting it, so that
without being able to do a thing to stop herself, Bobbie
discovered that she had raised her own arms to wrap
them tightly around Luke as she opened her mouth to
the demanding pressure of his probing tongue, that the
anger fuelling her was making her body ache and yearn,
that the low growl of sound Luke made deep in his throat
as she raked his tongue passionately with her teeth and
pushed herself even closer to his body so that she could
feel the powerful surge of male arousal that jolted
through him, made her emit a small, purring, femininely
feline sound of triumphant pleasure of her own.

As she felt his hands on her body, a fierce, wild thrill
of hunger swept through her, banishing logic and reason
and even reality; they were man and woman, yin and
yang, cause and effect, two primitive forces that when
combined together…

When Bobbie felt Luke's hand covering her breast,
pushing aside her clothes with savage urgency to reach
the soft warmth of her flesh, she moaned a sharp protest
beneath her breath, but the protest wasn't because he was
touching her. She was trembling from head to foot, the
sheer force of the desire that had erupted inside her from

out of nowhere making her body ache with something approaching an actual physical pain.

She had never dreamt that physical desire could generate such an intense and immediate reaction, such a sense of urgency and aching, teeth-grinding immediacy.

'Luke...' She neither knew nor cared what she might be betraying as she dragged her mouth from his to whisper his name in female need, the look in her eyes as they met his, his flashing a message of intense pride and equally intense desire.

She could see Luke's response in the way his pupils dilated, feel it in the unexpected tremor that passed through his body as he responded as though by telepathy to the need conveyed in her husky moaning of his name to run the hard pad of his thumb over the soft curve of her breast until he found her nipple and then to circle it and go on circling it as Bobbie gasped her physical pleasure in his touch and instinctively pressed herself even closer to him. And she could hear it in the harsh sound of the air escaping from his lungs as he muttered something unintelligible under his breath and then, leaning back against the wall, urged her between his parted thighs. Then, under the protective shadows, he dragged her clothes completely free of her breast so that he could satisfy the need pounding through both their tormented bodies by fastening his mouth over the swollen point of her nipple and sucking rhythmically on it.

It was the sound of a child crying in the hallway outside that broke the dark spell that was binding them together, causing them to spring apart and watch one another breathing harshly, confronting one another not as lovers but as warriors, foes, enemies, Bobbie recognised sickly as she tried to come to terms with what had happened, what she had done.

Denied the physical protection of the warmth of Luke's body and the emotional and mental protection of the sheer heat of the need that had possessed her, Bobbie started to shiver.

Luke's face was hidden from her by the shadows, not that she wanted to look at him, to see the contemptuous triumph she was sure must be in his eyes. No matter how much one might deplore it, there was still this un-spoken belief that whilst it was still just acceptable for a man to be motivated by and give in to sexual desire, where a woman was concerned the waters were far more muddied and dangerous. Bobbie wasn't even sure herself which side of the fence *she* stood on. Certainly she would never condemn another woman for admitting that she felt only physical desire and lust for a man, but when that woman was herself... She pushed away the idea that love could be tangled up in her emotions.

'I hate you, do you know that?' she told Luke huskily, adjusting her top before she opened the door and walked shakily through it—and away from him—moving down the hallway blindly to mingle with the other guests, her fists clenched as she fought to suppress her emotions, coming only to a halt when she realised she had reached the far side of the drawing room and could go no farther.

'So you're the American I've been hearing so much about.'

As Bobbie turned her head, she saw that there was someone seated in the wing-chair next to the window, a man in his seventies whom she had no difficulty what-soever in guessing to be Ben Crighton.

'I imagine so,' she concurred warily.

'Hah. Been telling you about me, have they? Warning you!' he exclaimed with a dry laugh.

'It has been mentioned that you don't particularly care for my countrymen,' Bobbie agreed calmly.

'They were over here during the war. Caused a lot of trouble, a lot of resentment, turning women's heads whilst their own men were away fighting.'

Bobbie forced herself not to make any kind of response, instead simply listening.

'You're looking after young Amelia, so I hear,' Ben commented gruffly.

'For the time being,' Bobbie returned.

'Joss said he met you in the churchyard looking at the gravestones, our gravestones.... Interested in us, are you?'

'You're a very…interesting family,' was all Bobbie allowed herself to be provoked into saying.

'Saw you talking to young Max earlier.'

Bobbie waited, expecting to be told once again that Max was a married man, but to her surprise, Ben didn't refer to Max's marriage at all.

'He's the image of my son, David…always was,' he related instead. 'Much more like him than his own father. Same character…'

Bobbie said nothing. From what she had heard about David, Olivia's father, she doubted that she would have liked him very much.

'He's abroad at the moment....'

Bobbie had no idea why she should be swept by compassion for a man she barely knew and who, from what she had heard, was as obstinate, narrow-minded and bigoted as any man could be. But whatever the reason, instead of pointing out that his son David was abroad—period—having simply disappeared in the night, leaving his family to deal with the havoc his disappearance had caused, she continued to say nothing.

The silence between them was only broken when Jenny suddenly appeared at her side, announcing, 'Bobbie, there's a telephone call for you…your sister…she sounded…' She touched Bobbie's arm gently. 'She said she needed to speak with you urgently. You can take the call in the study. You'll be private in there.'

Her mouth dry with apprehension, Bobbie followed

Jenny as she weaved her way through the throng, her heart thudding nervously as Jenny guided her across the hallway and pushed open the door to a small, cosy room almost filled by a huge desk.

As Jenny gently closed the door and left, Bobbie walked over to the desk and picked up the telephone receiver, saying uncertainly, 'Sam…?'

'Bobbie. Thank the Lord. Listen, have you said anything yet?'

'No…no, not yet. Sam, why are you calling me here? Is it Mom?'

'No, or at least not in the way you mean. She's okay. Look, Bobbie, you've got to do it today, confront *her*, show her, show them.'

'Sam,' Bobbie protested, 'it isn't that easy…I…'

'Bobbie, you've *got* to, *that's* why I'm ringing. Dad's on to us and—'

'What?'

'Now don't panic. Just listen up, will you? He found out I'd been ringing you in Chester, and you know Dad. He put two and two together and came up with four. He grilled me like he was one of his own Secret Service gorillas,' she told Bobbie indignantly.

'Oh, Sam, no…' Bobbie had to sit down. Her legs, her whole body, had gone weak with shock and stress. She sank into the comfortable leather swivel chair behind the desk and clutched the receiver. 'What did he say?'

'Oh, you know Pop. There was a lot of idealistic stuff about how we should be above wanting to make others pay for their errors. How it should be simply enough for us to be aware of them and to feel sorry for them because of the way they are. He said that nothing we would do could make things any easier for Mom, and then Grandpa had to get in on the act and he said—'

'Grandpa!' Bobbie interrupted her twin on a stifled gasp. 'Oh, Sam, no... How did Grandpa find out?'

'He came in while Dad was reading me the Riot Act,' Samantha confessed, 'and of course, he had to hear the whole thing. Anyway, I told them it was too late to do anything now and I told them what you were going to do and—'

There was a sharp click on the telephone line as though someone had picked up another handset.

Nervously Bobbie asked her sister, 'What was that? Has someone come in...Dad or...?'

'No. There's no one else here,' Samantha assured her. 'We're not going to give up, Bobbie, not now. We can't afford to. She's got to be made to pay.'

Bobbie bit her lip. She had never been totally happy with her twin's plans but weakly she had allowed herself to be persuaded into going along with them. Knowing now that her father and her grandfather had discovered what they were doing brought home to her how much they would both dislike and disapprove of Samantha's scheme.

'Bobbie,' she heard her sister warning her grimly, before pausing and then telling her bitterly, 'Look, over fifty years ago, Ruth Crighton pretended that she'd fallen in love with Grandpa and even promised to marry him. He believed her, they were lovers and then he got a message—not from her, mind you—but from her father via his own commanding officer announcing that Ruth never wanted to see him again, and when he tried to telephone her to talk to her, she told him that it was true and that she wanted nothing more to do with him.

'No explanations were given, no reasons, no apologies, but worse than that, a thousand times worse, she never even told him that she was already carrying his child. She simply took herself off to the other side of the country, gave birth to Grandpa's baby, *our* mother, in secret, and then walked away...walked away... abandoned Mom totally, leaving her to be given away for adoption like...like an unwanted kitten.

'If Grandpa hadn't been visiting an injured airman in that same hospital, if he hadn't happened to overhear two nurses gossiping about "that poor little motherless Crighton baby" and made enquiries, he would never even have known that Mom existed. When I think of what might have happened to her, it makes my blood run cold.

'You know what a hard time Grandpa had convincing first his commanding officers and then the British authorities that he was Mom's father and that he had a right to bring her up himself. You know the hardship that both he and Mom suffered when he first brought her back to this country. How first his family treated her and then Pop's. You *know* what it's done to Mom, knowing that her own mother didn't want her...that she hadn't even left so much as a letter for her...a note...anything...so that at least Mom could have felt that she had been loved by her...that she hadn't wanted to part with her. It's like Mom says. It's not just the fact that she's never known her mother that hurts. What hurts much, much more is that Ruth has never, ever wanted to know her...that she's never, ever tried to find her, to make even the most basic enquiries to find out what happened to her.'

'It was a very difficult time, Sam,' Bobbie told her sister in a low voice. 'The end of the war. British servicemen were coming home. Perhaps Ruth felt guilty about the fact that she'd been involved with an American. She had been engaged to someone else and...well, as Mom always says, she couldn't have had a more loving father or been a more loved child.'

'So guilty that she abandoned her own child? That's some guilt,' Samantha told Bobbie bitterly. 'Pity she hasn't felt even a quarter of it for what she did to Mom.

We have to see this through, Bobbie. She has to be made to pay…she deserves to pay. We agreed….'

Bobbie was just about to try to convince her sister that they should abandon their plan when the study door opened. Her eyes widened in shock as she saw Luke striding towards her. It wasn't so much the total unexpectedness of his appearance that left her speechless and virtually unable to move as he snatched the receiver from her hand and slammed it down, cutting her off from Samantha, as the look of murderously cold fury in his eyes.

'So, *you're* going to make Ruth *pay*, are you,' he demanded, thin-lipped as he took hold of her upper arm in a painfully hard grip. 'I don't think so. I don't think so at all. In fact, what I think you are going to do right now is to leave.'

'Leave…?' Bobbie protested squeakily. 'But—'

'My God, I was right about you all along, wasn't I?' Luke charged, overriding her nervous protest. 'But even *I* hadn't realised just how…how much you were going to demand from Ruth to keep quiet about her past.' His mouth twisted as though soured by something foul tasting.

'Blackmail… In my book it's the shabbiest, meanest, most heartless crime of them all, but I suppose I shouldn't be shocked. After all, it's not the first time I've come across it, although thankfully the closest contact I've had to have with the perpetrator has been when I've refused to handle his defence.'

'Blackmail!' Bobbie's eyes rounded with horror. 'Luke. You've got it all wrong—' she started to deny it but then broke off to wince in helpless protest as his angry grip on her upper arm tightened as he swung her round to face him.

'No. *You've* got it wrong,' he contradicted her flatly, 'and if I were you, I shouldn't bother wasting my breath trying to convince me otherwise, Bobbie. I'm not quite that much of a fool. Come on…this way….'

To Bobbie's chagrin, she found that she was actually being compelled to walk and, in fact, almost run as he positively dragged her out of the room and down the corridor in the opposite direction she had originally come.

'Let me go…what are you *doing*? Where are you taking me?' she protested in panic as she tried in vain to wriggle free.

'Let you go? No way, and as for what I'm doing…I'm doing what I should have done the first time I met you if I'd had any sense,' he told her grimly, stopping so abruptly in front of a small, almost invisible door set into the wall that Bobbie cannoned painfully into him.

When he opened it, Bobbie saw that it led into the garden. Her legs shook with relief. For one awful moment she had actually wondered…dreaded… feared…that he might be going to imprison her somewhere.

'This way,' he instructed, yanking her round and virtually marching her along a narrow path. Beyond the hedge in front of them, she could just make out the glimmer of car roofs.

Without giving her the chance to say anything, Luke forced her across to his own car, using his body as well as his constraining arm to imprison her between the car and himself as he unlocked the passenger door.

'Get in,' he told her curtly.

'Well now, what's going on here? No prizes for guessing why you two are sneaking off. I wonder…?'

Relief flooded through Bobbie as she recognised Max strolling towards them, but before she could open her mouth to ask him for help, Luke had all but pushed her into the passenger seat of the car and was shutting the door on her.

'Roberta isn't feeling very well,' she heard Luke telling Max in a distant voice. 'Tell Olivia not to worry and that I'll take care of her, will you, Max? Oh, and give your grandfather my apologies, as well.'

As Luke started to walk round to the driver's side of his car, Bobbie tried to push open the passenger door and call out to Max, who was now disappearing in the direction of the house. She found that Luke had locked her in, and even as her shaky fingers tried to activate the electric windows, she realised that they wouldn't operate without the ignition key. Then Luke was opening the door and sliding into the car beside her, setting it in motion with the doors already relocked and leaving her no alternative but to stay where she was.

'You have no right to do this,' she finally managed to say as he swung the car out onto the main road. 'You're kidnapping me and that's a crime and—'

'So's blackmail,' Luke countered tightly, 'and as for my kidnapping you...we're lovers...an item...an accredited couple...remember?'

The aggressively angry way in which Luke was driving the car caused Bobbie to be thrown back against her seat, the jolt making her gasp for breath, but it wasn't that that made it impossible for her to respond to Luke's taunt. She was still in shock from hearing him accuse her of wanting to blackmail Ruth.

'You can't do this, Luke,' she warned him, but the sideways glance of derision he gave her made her heart bang heavily against her chest.

'Who's going to stop me?' he scoffed. 'Your partner in crime?' He shook his head and laughed mirthlessly. 'I think not, and besides, you didn't leave me much option. After I'd heard what the nasty, cold-blooded little pair of you were planning, I knew I had to act swiftly to protect Ruth.'

Since that one statement encompassed three errors on

which she urgently needed to take issue with him, it was, as Bobbie was forced to acknowledge later, rather odd that it should be the least important of them she should protest to him about first, telling him shakily, 'We are not little and I resent your use of that kind of demeaning and discriminative language, especially when—'

'Oh please,' Luke interrupted her savagely. 'Spare me at least the politically correct whinge. My God, you really are in a class of your own, aren't you?' Luke breathed aggrievedly. 'You haven't a scrap of conscience about what you were planning to do, the hurt you were about to inflict, and yet you've got the gall to come on to me about calling you little…for all the world as though you're the wronged party.'

'I am,' Bobbie insisted fiercely. 'And how dare you talk to me about conscience. You must have deliberately listened in on our conversation. A private conversation…'

'Only accidentally,' Luke told her tersely. '*I* wanted to make a phone call of my own and had no idea the line was already in use until I picked up the receiver—'

'At which point any normal, decent person would have replaced it,' Bobbie rebuked him smartly, 'not eavesdropped.'

'For Ruth's sake, I had no other option,' Luke returned grimly. 'And thank God I did. How much were you intending to blackmail her for? Not that it matters— be it one penny or a million pounds, the concept is still the same.'

'We were not planning to blackmail Ruth,' Bobbie denied angrily. 'You've got it all wrong.'

'No, you're the one who's got it all wrong,' Luke replied acidly. 'Just how wrong you're about to find out….'

They were heading for Chester, Bobbie noticed. Inwardly she was quaking with apprehension and a sick sense of aching disillusionment.

Why on earth did she have to be such an idealistic and romantic fool? Now was quite definitely not the time to have herself mentally and emotionally confronting the fact that a small, deep and very secret feminine place within her had hoped against hope that if Luke were to be told the truth he would instantly and unhesitatingly share her feelings and not just share them, but also want to champion them, to champion *her*, she admitted; to love her so unequivocally and totally that he immediately and completely understood the complexity of her emotions.

But then, of course, Luke did *not* love her, did he? And if she was honest with herself, she had already known that.

'Where are you taking me?' she demanded as she firmly closed the door on her foolish dreams.

'Somewhere where you won't get the chance to put your nasty little plan into action—where you won't get the chance to make any contact with Ruth at all, somewhere where I can keep an eye on you until I can make arrangements to get you sent back where you came from.'

'What! Sent *back*...? You can't do *that*.'

'No? Even in this country we can and do deport undesirable aliens.'

Undesirable aliens! Bobbie took a deep breath and then counted to ten before saying coolly, 'I appreciate that your massive ego, your superiority complex and sense of justice give you the delusion that you can do whatever you like, Luke, but unfortunately for you and fortunately for me you are just as subject to the laws of the land as I am myself and not even *you* can have me forcibly imprisoned or forcibly repatriated just because it's what you want.'

Luke gave her a look that turned her blood to ice as he warned her, 'Don't tempt me. If that's a challenge you've just issued, then consider it taken up. The prison *I* have in mind for you may not be Chester gaol but rather my flat, and as for your repatriation, well, let's just say I am sure I shall be able to think of some way to encourage you to *want* to return home....'

Bobbie dared not look at him.

'You must think a lot of Ruth to go to all this trouble on her behalf,' Bobbie offered shakily.

'Yes, I do,' Luke agreed calmly, 'but it wouldn't matter *who* you were trying to blackmail. My reaction would be the same. If that's the kind of behaviour you've been brought up to think of as the norm, then no wonder Ruth dumped your grandfather.'

Bobbie stared at him in silence for several seconds, not because shock had deprived her of the ability to respond but because of the sheer weight and intensity of her fury.

When she did speak, she spaced her words carefully and slowly, reminding herself that there was nothing to be achieved in doing what she most wanted to do, which was to scream at him and beat her fists against his chest as she forced him to take back his insults.

'My *grandfather* and my *parents*,' she began and then had to stop because her voice had started to tremble so much her mouth could barely shape the words. '*You* aren't fit to be in the same room with them,' she told him shakily when she could speak. 'To breathe the same air...to exist in the same universe.'

'Abused children often display an intense degree of loyalty towards their parents. It's a phenomenon social workers often remark on,' Luke said brusquely. 'Apparently it's because they don't know any other way of relating, any other kind of relationship.'

'*My* parents…my *family*, are not child abusers,' Bobbie denied furiously. 'You don't understand….'

'I understand perfectly,' Luke corrected her flatly. 'After all, I heard your sister telling you that Ruth had to be made to pay.'

'To pay for abandoning our mother, yes,' Bobbie protested, 'but not to pay in *financial* terms. What we meant—'

'Don't waste your time lying to me, Bobbie,' Luke warned her coldly as he negotiated a difficult turning.

They were in Chester now and Bobbie realised with a sinking heart that there was every possibility that he would be able to carry out his threat and incarcerate her in his flat. But he couldn't keep her there for ever. Sooner or later he would have to leave her on her own and when he did…

Fiercely she started to make plans. If it came to the worst, she would just have to phone Sam and…

She tensed as she realised that Luke had stopped the car. Instinctively she reached for the door but Luke gave her a warning look and told her softly, 'I shouldn't bother making a run for it if I were you. I used to play rugger and I promise you that if I have to I'm quite willing to bring you down in the kind of tackle that could do a lot of expensive damage to those perfect teeth of yours.'

'My teeth happen to be my own, thank you very much, and not the result of some expensive cosmetic dentistry,' Bobbie responded sharply, tilting her chin at him so that he would know that she wasn't in the least bit intimidated by his threat.

Even so, she decided that it might not be a good idea to risk humiliating herself by trying to run away from him, remembering the ease with which he had constrained her earlier and, of course, the street was empty, which meant that there was no one she could call out to for help.

'You can't keep me here for ever,' she warned him ten minutes later after he had bundled her unceremoniously up the entry stairs and into his surprisingly spacious and elegant living quarters above the firm's offices. 'For a start, Olivia is bound to want to know what's going on. I am supposed to be working for her after all....'

'I can promise you that keeping you here for ever is the last thing on my mind,' Luke assured her unkindly, 'and as for Olivia... Well, I think she will understand when I explain to her that the pair of us were just so overcome by our emotions that we had to be together. Just as she'll also understand why you decided you had to return home once we had decided that our...er... passion for one another had worn itself out.'

Bobbie stared at him. 'You've got it all planned out, haven't you?' she accused him, 'but you've still got it all wrong.'

'So you keep protesting,' Luke agreed coldly, 'but I'm sure you'll understand when I say that you just aren't convincing me.'

'No, I don't,' Bobbie objected spiritedly. 'Isn't there a law in this country that says a person is presumed innocent until proven guilty? You *want* me to be guilty, Luke, and that's why you've already prejudged me. You *want* to think the worst of me. You want to believe that I'm...I'm...'

'A blackmailer,' Luke supplied relentlessly for her. 'You condemned yourself with your own words, Bobbie.'

'That was a private conversation,' she told him angrily, 'and one that you've completely misinterpreted. Ruth abandoned my mother when she was less than a couple of days old. Have you *any* idea what that meant?

No, of course you haven't. My mother was rejected at birth by her own mother—totally and completely abandoned. Something like that hurts and goes on hurting all through a person's life....'

'And so *you* decided to make Ruth hurt, as well, but through her bank account rather than her emotions,' Luke taunted her cynically.

'No, that's not true,' Bobbie denied fiercely. 'Ruth *is* my grandmother,' she reminded him. 'You surely don't think...'

'The grandmother who didn't want you, who rejected your grandfather and your mother,' Luke pointed out cruelly. 'In a world where it isn't unknown for children to murder their parents to get their hands on their money, why should I believe that you have any warm feelings for Ruth, why should anyone? In fact—'

'You want to believe the worst of me,' Bobbie cried out passionately. 'You've been antagonistic towards me, suspicious of me, right from the start.'

'With good reason,' Luke told her curtly. 'As it happens, it never occurred to me that you might be a potential blackmailer but I did rather wonder, in view of your suspicious curiosity about the history of our family, if you were thinking of attempting a similar bogus claim as a client of mine was subjected to last year when someone turned up claiming to be his illegitimate son.

'Fortunately we were able to prove that his claim was totally fictitious, but the stress of what he was put through caused my client to suffer some acute anxiety and it also placed a great deal of strain on his marriage since this young man was claiming that he had actually been conceived during the early years of the marriage.'

'It does happen,' Bobbie observed.

'Maybe, but in my view that isn't any justification for the havoc that the result of some unfortunate liaison can cause.'

'The *result*. You're talking about human beings,' Bobbie told him passionately. '*People* with *feelings*...with *needs*, with *emotions*...but, of course, that's something you wouldn't know anything about, isn't it?' she flung at him furiously.

'On the contrary, I know exactly what it means,' Luke corrected her softly.

An electric tension suddenly seemed to have filled the room, making it difficult for Bobbie to breathe properly. She could hear the rapid shallowness of her own breathing and was even more conscious of the heavy unevenness of Luke's making an agonizingly sensual counterpoint to her own.

She could see a small betraying pulse beat under Luke's skin as he hardened his jaw and, like a forest fire spreading over dry, desperately thirsty timber, all it took was the merest breath of air, the smallest indrawn breath, to fan and spread the dangerous flames Bobbie could feel leaping so fiercely to life inside her; all that was needed was the merest spark to set alight the raging conflagration of passion they had shared earlier, and for her, in making that verbal reference to it, Luke had supplied that spark.

Hungrily she focused on his mouth and was unable to make herself look away. Think about Mom, then about Sam...think about how Luke has insulted you, misjudged you...hurt you, she warned herself, but it was no use. The fire was already burning out of control and she was consumed by it and with the searing heat of her own need—a need she knew instinctively that Luke shared.

'My God, you know what you're inviting...inciting...don't you?' Luke warned her rawly, but he was still coming towards her, closing the gap between them, taking hold of her with the same bruising grip he had used earlier but which they both knew had nothing to do with wanting to imprison or hurt her.

Bobbie didn't even try to escape or move. She simply stood there watching...waiting...*knowing*...

'You realise that this time I'm not going to be *able* to stop, don't you?' Luke told her thickly. 'You *know* what's going to happen between us...what's destined to happen between us....'

'You hate me,' Bobbie reminded him, making a last feeble bid to drag them both back to sanity and reality.

'Yes,' Luke agreed bleakly, 'I hate you. I hate myself, too. In fact, I loathe and despise the pair of us. You, and myself even more so for knowing what you are and yet still wanting you. *Wanting* you,' he groaned and then said savagely, 'Dear God, if only it were that simple. I shouldn't have brought you here!'

'Then let me go,' Bobbie said simply. She wasn't going to plead with him, to beg to be set free and besides... It was her pride that was stopping her from doing so, she assured herself heatedly. That was all. Her pride...nothing else and most certainly *not* the twisting, aching, crying need for him that was tormenting her so painfully.

'I can't,' Luke told her broodingly, focusing abruptly on her as he added, 'You know that and you know why....'

'Because...because of Ruth,' Bobbie whispered, her mouth suddenly dry, her heart pounding with heavy, slow strokes that made her feel breathless and light-headed.

She stiffened as Luke's tortured gaze dropped to her mouth. He lifted his hand and dragged the hard pad of his thumb along her bottom lip.

The sensation of the slight roughness of his skin moving against the sensitive flesh of her mouth, already swollen from the passionate kisses they had exchanged

at Queensmead, made Bobbie's whole body shiver in
sensual pleasure—a reaction which she knew Luke had
to have registered.

His thumb stopped moving, the air between them so
charged with their mutual tension that Bobbie could
hardly breathe.

'You do know what you're doing to me, don't you?'
Luke demanded roughly before his head came down.

Instinctively Bobbie tried to protect herself from what
she knew was going to happen, trying to sink her teeth
into his thumb in a defensive action born out of panic;
only instead of withdrawing from her in angry pain,
Luke pressed his thumb deeper into her mouth, caressing
the soft, swollen, exquisitely responsive inner flesh of
her lip.

'Look at me,' Bobbie heard him commanding her
rawly. 'Look at me and see what you're doing to me.'
She battled and failed to control the soft moan of tormented pleasure that escaped her. 'Look at me, Bobbie.'

Helplessly she did so, her own eyes widening in
shocked recognition of the desire, the arousal, the
fiercely male pleasure she could see burning so darkly
in his eyes.

It was impossible for her to look away, impossible,
too, for her to prevent *him* from seeing in her own expression her feminine counterpoint to his arousal.

Weakly she gave in to the need overpowering her,
touching his flesh with the tip of her tongue, savouring
the taste and texture of it before wantonly drawing it
deeper into her mouth, stroking and sucking on his
thumb with a rhythmic urgency she was far, far beyond
controlling.

Through the heat haze of her own passion, she heard
Luke mutter something beneath his breath and then he
was kissing her mouth with the kind of passion that sent
her own body into a tumultuous response, wrapping his

arms around her and still kissing her; picking her up and carrying her through to the bedroom.

Bobbie had a vague impression of cool neutral colours and natural fabrics, a large bed with polished wooden headboard and footboard, a couple of matching, very masculine chests, the clean, fresh smell of cedar warmed by sandalwood as though the creamily soft bedlinen had been stored in an antique armoire.

As he laid her on the bed, Bobbie could see the entwined initials embroidered onto the pillows, a legacy, no doubt, from some past Crighton's bride's lovingly prepared dowry.

'I shouldn't be doing this. It goes against everything I've ever believed in, everything I've been—'

'Then stop! Stop now and let me go,' Bobbie interrupted Luke wildly as she lay imprisoned beneath him, his hands framing her face as he searched her face.

He gave her an unkind smile.

'Is that really what you want?' he tormented her, lifting one hand to deliberately trace a line downwards from the hollow of her throat between her breasts.

Dear God! She could almost *see*, never mind *feel*, her breasts swelling and straining upwards in wanton and urgent demand for his touch—and not just the touch of his hands, she acknowledged as he bent his head and slowly started to use his mouth to follow the path of his tormenting finger.

She could feel herself starting to tremble violently. The scent of his skin, his hair, of *him*, filled her nostrils like some kind of black-magic aphrodisiac.

'Luke…' She moaned his name, a soft, keening sound of female need, closing her eyes and arching her body, quiveringly, achingly, desperately trying to cling on to the self-control she could feel slipping away from her and carrying her along with all the momentum and danger of a mountain avalanche.

She could feel the warmth of his breath against her skin through her clothes and had to fight the sharp urge to slide her fingers into his hair and urge him closer to her body. He was kissing the space between the buttons fastening her top, his mouth pushing aside the fabric as he played on her tormented body and overstrung emotions, deliberately tantalising and tormenting her, she felt sure.

But she was gone way, way beyond the point where she could summon pride and common sense or even dignity to halt the landslide, the shocking swiftness of her descent into the dark realm of her almost violent demanding needs and when Luke's hand reached out to cover her breast over her clothes she cried out harshly in longing to have him touch her more intimately, to have him satisfy the hunger, the urgency she felt for skin-on-skin contact.

She wanted him so much that she didn't even realise what she was doing as she started to tug frantically at her top.

'What is it...what do you want?' she heard Luke demanding hoarsely as his hand covered her own and held it fast against her body, trapping it and her as he looked deep into her eyes. 'Tell me, Bobbie,' he insisted thickly. 'Tell me...I want to hear you say it....'

Bobbie licked her dry lips with the tip of her tongue, shuddering as she felt the fierce lick of the inner flames burning through her. 'I want *you*, Luke...I want you to...'

'Yes...you want me to what?' he asked her rawly. 'You want me to tear every stitch of clothing from your body and leave it...you...naked to *me*...to my eyes... my hands...my mouth...?'

Bobbie moaned, trembling intensely, unable to stop herself from reacting, not just to what he was saying to her and the mental images he was conjuring up for her, but to what she could see in his eyes, as well, the message he was so clearly giving her that whilst he might verbally be playing the protagonist and pretending that he was aloof from the need that burned through her and fully in control of himself and her, the truth was that he had as little control over what was happening and his own fiercely male response to it as she had herself.

And perhaps that was why instead of fighting him, clawing her way back to reality and resisting everything he was offering her, everything she knew she so badly wanted, everything she knew *he* so badly wanted, she let him see in her eyes exactly what she was feeling, exactly what she was needing, exactly what the passionate, explosive, annihilating blend of physical desire and angry emotion was doing to her.

'Yes. Yes. I want all of that...and more, much more...more....' she admitted huskily, wildly, giving in to the dangerous thrill of not just going with the speeding avalanche but actively pushing it, increasing its velocity, its power. Somewhere, way, way below her, trauma and pain awaited her but at this moment all she cared about was the shocking, hitherto unknown, all-consuming excitement of being exposed to so much danger, of being a part of it, co-responsible for it, of knowing, despite what Luke was trying to imply, that all she had to do to *make* him join her in her self-created descent to destruction was to reach up, yes, as she was doing right now, and start unfastening the buttons of his shirt. Not all of them...not yet...just enough for her to be able to slide her hands inside his shirt so that she could caress the hard bones of his shoulders whilst her tongue tip explored the hollow of his throat and then moved upwards to caress his jaw.

She heard him groan, felt the reverberation of the low, tormented sound he couldn't withhold all the way down to her toes and knew that now he would do it, now he would do exactly what he had threatened as she felt the hands he had used to imprison her tugging feverishly at her clothes, trembling against her skin as he unfastened and pulled down her top, exposing her breasts to the late-afternoon sunlight so that they were gilded with its warmth.

'Oh God. Milk and honey,' she thought she heard him mutter as he cupped them both and then rubbed the pads of his thumbs over and over her nipples until she lost control completely and could only hear herself crying out pleadingly to him that she wanted, needed, *had* to feel the heat, the touch of his mouth against them. 'Like this?' he demanded rawly.

But she couldn't make any response. All she could do was to hold the back of his head in her hands and look down at his dark hair as he lay against her breast and the hot, urgent tug of his mouth on her nipple sent a jolt of sensation hot-wiring all the way from the centre of her breast to the heart of her womb. Instinctively her thighs parted, her body arching, a shocked cry leaving her lips as she realised what was going to happen.

Luke knew it, too. She could tell by the way he was looking at her as he reluctantly released her breast to look into her face whilst he still nuzzled its swollen temptation.

'This shouldn't be happening.' Bobbie hadn't realised she had spoken the words out loud until she felt Luke's hands travelling lower down her body. 'No,' she protested, but they both knew her denial wasn't of him or his touch but of her own response to it.

'Take me now…take me now, Bobbie,' she heard him whispering hoarsely to her. 'You *know* you want to. You know you're *ready* to.'

She didn't make any verbal response. She couldn't. Both of them were shaking as he removed the rest of their clothes, and when she saw him looking at her,

Bobbie wanted desperately to be able to hold on to the moment, to lie proudly beneath his gaze, all female. She wanted to have the time to do her own share of gazing, to subject his naked body to as uninhibited and erotic a scrutiny as he did to hers, but she couldn't. Quite simply, they didn't have the time. *She* didn't have the time and the feeling that engulfed her as she saw that he was ready for her turned the whole of her insides to liquid heat.

His first thrust made her clench her teeth to try to stop herself from grinding them together in frustration, it was so slow and careful.

She wanted to urge him to move faster, deeper, to ride the wave of her desire for him as it crested but then she forgot what it was she had been about to say…to demand…as he started to thrust once more, swiftly, deeply, once, twice and then again, and just as she was beginning to pick up his rhythm, returning to his earlier slower movement.

It was torment, torture, an unbearable white hell of sensation so acutely pleasurable that she wanted to scream with the exquisite ecstasy of it. But quite simply, there wasn't time. Even as she opened her mouth the wave broke, sending them both crashing through the foam-speckled, churningly fierce, white-water rapids of their mutual desire.

She heard Luke cry out, the sound of a man in mortal agony or immortal ecstasy, and then, shockingly, shudderingly, it was over.

When Bobbie opened her eyes, the bedroom was in darkness. It took her several seconds to remember where she was and why. She had fallen so quickly and so deeply asleep after…after…afterwards, that her body was still curved with feminine vulnerability next to Luke's. Not that she could have moved away from him even if she had wanted to, at least not without waking him up, because one very powerful male thigh—one very powerful, naked male thigh—was thrown across her body, anchoring her to the bed and to him.

Even though she hadn't moved, something must have alerted Luke to the fact that she was awake because suddenly she felt the change in the tempo of his warm breath against the nape of her neck. His hand stroked slowly down her naked arm and then up again, coming to rest against her bare breast. Tiny quivers of sensation flooded her body, tiny pinpoint darts of pleasure emanating from the vulnerable place below her ear that he was caressing so slowly and deliciously with his mouth.

'Turn round,' she heard him instructing her softly. 'I want to kiss you properly.'

This time the build-up was more leisurely, the caresses he bestowed on her body and she on his, with both their hands and their lips, more intimate and prolonged, but the final outcome was the same—an explosion of white-hot passion that engulfed the two of them, causing them to cry out and cling to one another as the full flood of their shared need ripped through them both.

CHAPTER SEVEN

THE next time Bobbie opened her eyes, it was daylight and she was on her own. As the memories of the physical intimacy and oneness they had shared and the emotional intimacy and commitment they had not came back to her, she closed her eyes and wept silent tears of pain and grief. Pain for the hurt she knew lay ahead of her, and grief for the loss, the stillbirth, of the love she knew she could simply never allow to exist and that certainly did not exist for Luke.

The neatly embroidered, entwined initials on the pillowcase caught her eye. Carefully she traced them with the tip of her finger, the same gently stroking touch of exploration she had used on Luke's body last night.

This bedlinen had been embroidered by a long ago Crighton bride. A Crighton bride! That was something, *someone*, *she* would never be. Hot tears burned the back of her eyelids. Where was Luke? She must not let him see her like this and suspect what she was feeling.

What she was feeling... What *was* she feeling? Did she really need to ask herself? Hadn't her reaction to him, to last night, already told her, forced her to confront the truth she had been avoiding and trying to suppress virtually from the moment they met? She was in love with him; she loved him.

She closed her eyes and swallowed hard, a small sound of anguish bubbling in her throat. No, not that, she couldn't, she must not... Where was her *pride*? Her self-respect, her sense of self-worth and self-preservation?

And where, too, was Luke?

The flat felt oddly empty. But surely he wouldn't have left her here alone to make her escape.... Not after what he had said to her yesterday. Not after the threats he had made, the fury he had exhibited.

Cautiously she swung her legs out of the bed, and wrapping the duvet around her to cover her nudity, she padded over to the bedroom door and opened it.

'Luke...?'

No answer.

She froze as someone suddenly began knocking urgently on the outer door. Whilst she hesitated, wondering whether or not to answer it, she heard Olivia's voice calling through the door.

'Bobbie. Quick, let me in.'

When she unlocked the door, Olivia practically fell through it. She looked flushed and slightly on edge, Bobbie noticed, as though she was excited, and she hardly seemed to register Bobbie's state of undress or the fact that she was on her own.

'Look, you've got to get dressed,' she commanded quickly, 'and please hurry. I can't explain now.'

'What...?' Bobbie started to protest, but Olivia was already urging her back towards the bedroom.

'No, don't ask me,' she said. 'I can't explain now. But you must hurry. Please...'

Still hesitating, Bobbie asked her uncertainly, 'Is this...is it Luke?'

'This has nothing to do with Luke,' Olivia answered her, adding in some surprise as she finally realised he wasn't there, 'Where is he, by the way?'

'I don't know,' Bobbie replied honestly.

'Oh well, I'm afraid we haven't time to wait for him,' Olivia told her determinedly, 'even though I know you probably want to.'

Want to? Her? If only Olivia knew...

'No...that's right,' she responded shakily, going up to

retrieve the clothes still scattered around the bedroom and blushingly glad that Olivia hadn't come with her to see how they had been flung all over the place.

Whilst Olivia paced the sitting room, Bobbie quickly showered and dressed, then went to join Olivia, saying nervously that she must look dreadful without any make-up.

'You look wonderful,' Olivia told her, shaking her head and then urging, 'Come on, we must hurry....'

'Hurry where?' Bobbie wanted to know, but Olivia was already taking hold of her arm and impelling her towards the entrance door. She felt rather like someone in *Alice in Wonderland*, Bobbie decided dazedly, as Olivia rushed her down the stairs and outside into the bright sunlight.

Where was Luke? What was going on? *Why* was Olivia both so impatient and so excited at the same time and what...?

Bobbie came to an abrupt halt as she saw Ruth standing in the street not next to her own car but a huge polished Rover.

'Oh, Bobbie...' Emotionally Ruth hugged her as soon as Bobbie drew close to her and she could see tears shining in her eyes. Completely bewildered by what was happening, she watched as Ruth and Olivia exchanged emotional and highly charged looks.

'Quick, get in the car, both of you,' Olivia instructed, then asked Ruth, 'Are you sure you should be driving?'

'I'm sure,' Ruth assured her, giving her a wide but slightly wobbly smile and then hugging Olivia as she added, 'but I'm not sure—'

'Yes, you are,' Bobbie heard Olivia telling her firmly as she stepped back for her and Ruth opened the car door.

'Get in, darling,' Ruth instructed Bobbie.

Darling...? Bobbie's jaw dropped but Olivia was already opening the passenger door to the car and pushing Bobbie into the seat.

'Don't drive too fast,' she then warned Ruth.

'Will someone please tell me what is going on?' Bobbie begged.

'You'll find out soon enough,' Olivia told her mysteriously.

An awful thought suddenly struck Bobbie. What if Luke had enlisted Ruth and Olivia's aid and they were...? What? What could they do? Besides, one look at both their faces was enough to reassure Bobbie that whatever was going on, it had nothing to do with Luke's misinterpretation of the phone call he had overheard her having with Samantha.

No, whatever mystifying reason they had for their behaviour, it was obviously one that both of them found exciting. Bobbie gnawed on her bottom lip and then winced as she felt the pain in her still-tender, passionately kissed flesh. Olivia was excited, yes, but Ruth...

Ruth was more than simply excited; she had never seen the older woman behaving so emotionally before. And she had called her 'darling'. A slip of the tongue or...

'Ruth, will you please tell me what is going on?' she begged.

'I don't think I can,' Ruth responded. 'You'll see....' She placed her hand on her mouth and Bobbie could see that her eyes were suddenly bright with tears. 'I've promised that I... I can't...not yet.'

'Promised? Who?'

Bobbie's heart started to pound uncomfortably as Ruth negotiated the traffic and turned onto the motorway slip-road. They were heading for Manchester.

She could hardly bear to think now of what had happened the previous night. How could she ever face Luke again, knowing what he would be thinking...? Knowing how he would be gloating...? In fact, she would go to the farthest ends of the earth to prevent herself from having to do so...from having to look into his face, his eyes, and see there the record of his intimate knowledge of her weakness, her vulnerability, her *love* for him. For surely he must now be aware of it...he must know just what had motivated her passionate...her very passionate response to him.

For men, of course, it was different. Men did not... She tensed as she realised that Ruth was heading for the motorway exit marked Airport.

Airport...? *Was* Ruth taking her to the airport so that she...so that she could what? Bobbie didn't even have her passport with her.

What was going on...?

Frowningly Bobbie studied Ruth. She looked younger somehow, softer...and more vulnerable. Bobbie could smell the delicate light fragrance she always wore. Her hair looked as though it had just been styled, she noticed, and her nails gleamed with a soft pale polish. Ruth always looked elegant, but today... Today the soft vanilla-coloured silk casuals she was wearing looked as though they had come from an exclusive designer boutique, the soft shape of the skirt emphasising the fact that Ruth still had an enviably slender and youthful-looking body.

She looked, yes, she looked, Bobbie decided in surprise as the airport terminal buildings loomed ahead of them, like a woman who was dressed for a very special date—with a man!

But Ruth did not date, or at least not according to Olivia, and Bobbie had no reason to doubt her.

'Only a little while longer. Please, please be patient, dar...Bobbie,' Ruth implored her.

There it was again. Ruth had been about to call her 'darling' again. What on earth was going on?

Bobbie was desperate to know, but Ruth was driving

into the car park and asking Bobbie to tell her if she could see a vacant space.

Even once they had parked the car, Ruth still refused to tell Bobbie what was happening, demanding instead as she hurried them along towards the arrivals hall entrance, 'Come on…we haven't got much time.'

Ruth seemed as excited and as nervous as a young girl, Bobbie reflected. The years seemed to have dropped away from her, giving Bobbie a sudden and illuminating awareness of how she must have looked when she and her grandfather had first met. She thought she could even see in Ruth's animated expression a similarity to her own mother.

The passengers from the incoming flight were already starting to file through into the arrivals hall as Ruth rushed Bobbie towards the barrier, her grip on Bobbie's hand as she tugged her along so tight that Bobbie knew exactly how tense and anxious she was.

Automatically Bobbie studied the travel-weary passengers and then her eyes widened in disbelieving shock as she recognised four of them. What were her parents, her grandfather and sister doing here? She turned instinctively to Ruth for an explanation but Ruth was in no fit state to listen to her, never mind answer her, Bobbie recognised. Ruth's whole concentration was fixed on the tall, grey-haired, broad-shouldered man outstripping the walking pace of the rest of his family. As he reached the barrier he held out his arms, exclaiming emotionally, 'Ruth…my little Ruthie…'

'Grant…' Bobbie heard Ruth cry out with something suspiciously like a sob in her voice as she flung herself into Bobbie's grandfather's open arms.

Open-mouthed, Bobbie watched them embracing with all the fervour and lack of self-consciousness of two teenagers, holding one another, touching one another's faces as if they each couldn't quite believe the other was real, as they shared laughter and tears and low-voiced husky endearments, totally oblivious to family members and the curious and sentimentally sympathetic onlookers they were attracting.

As she watched them, Bobbie felt her own eyes smart with tears. This was how love should be. Not... She bit hard on her lip, reminding herself fiercely that Luke did not love her, while her grandfather...

'Oh, Grant, you haven't changed at all,' she heard Ruth saying emotionally.

'No, nor have you,' Grant returned softly as he cupped Ruth's face and studied each feature. 'You still look exactly like the girl I remember....'

'Oh, Grant,' Ruth protested shakily. 'I'm not that girl any longer. I'm—'

'You're the woman I love,' Grant interrupted her firmly. 'The woman I've *always* loved and always will love. The woman I'm too damned afraid to kiss properly here in public just in case I disgrace myself and embarrass her.'

'Oh, Grant,' Ruth breathed, her face suffused with colour.

'Well, it's the truth,' Grant told her unashamedly. 'It's been a hell of a long time, Ruthie, and there's never been anyone for me but you....'

'I still can't quite believe that this is really happening. That it's not just a dream,' Ruth told him tremulously. 'When Olivia said that Bobbie's grandfather was on the telephone and wanted to speak with me, I had no idea—'

'You'll never know how scared I was that you would just hang up on me,' Grant interrupted her softly. 'But once Sam had 'fessed up and told us what she and Bobbie were planning, I just knew we had to stop her and warn her.'

'I recognised your voice straight away,' Ruth offered shyly, 'but I still couldn't believe...'

'We've wasted so many years already. I don't want to waste the ones that are left. I can't afford to,' Grant told her humorously. 'I'm not a young man any more.'

'You are to me,' Ruth returned softly. She still couldn't take it all in. The shock of being asked to speak with Bobbie's grandfather and then discovering that he was Grant, *her* Grant—plus the other revelations that had followed that initial phone call—still hadn't entirely faded. She might have stuck to her promise to Grant not to say a word to Bobbie about what had happened or the imminent arrival of her family all the way to the airport but that hadn't stopped her from just aching to talk to Bobbie about him...about all of them, but most especially about Grant and, of course, about their child...*her* daughter, Bobbie and Samantha's mother.

She couldn't quite believe how wonderful Grant looked, tall and straight-backed, his hair silver. It was still thick and gleaming with health while his eyes were just as full as ever of warmth. And his smell...his touch...his kiss... She felt like a young girl again, only more so...because this time... Only, in reality, she wasn't a young girl and there were other factors, other people, involved in their relationship now, especially...

She looked with nervous longing beyond Grant to the stunningly beautiful, still red-haired woman who stood surrounded by her husband and daughters and yet at the same time slightly aloof from them.

Ruth bit her lip.

They had spoken on the phone, exchanged tears and explanations, but even so...

'Sarah Jane,'' she called out gently and then a little uncertainly held out her arms.

'Ruth...Mama...'

'Oh, my darling girl,' Ruth cried, closing her eyes on the tears burning them as she held her grown-up daughter in her arms, the daughter whom she had last held when she was only hours, days, old but who she could have sworn still had that same sweetly precious scent she had had as a baby…a scent Ruth knew she would have recognised anywhere out of a thousand, a hundred thousand, women.

And she had called her Mama. Not the American 'Mom' showing that that was how she thought of her or even that she had thought of her. Not that Ruth needed any confirmation of that, not after what Grant and Sarah Jane herself had told her in their transatlantic telephone conversations.

'Oh, my darling, darling girl,' Ruth whispered. 'How could you ever think I didn't want you…didn't love you.' She cupped Sarah Jane's face and looked deep into her eyes, telling her emotionally, 'There hasn't been a day when I haven't thought about you…or a night when I haven't said a prayer for your happiness and well-being…or when I haven't missed you and cried for you. Every birthday…every anniversary, I wondered and yearned to know you, thought about you and tried to send you a mental message of love. The only reason…the only reason I gave you up was because I genuinely believed that I was doing the best thing for you….'

Standing three feet away watching them, Bobbie felt her own eyes prick with tears. Her father, who was standing between her and Samantha, touched Bobbie lightly on the arm and said quietly, 'Come on, let's give them a few minutes together on their own and besides—'

'Besides, I want to know what's going on,' Bobbie interrupted him plaintively. 'Ruth wouldn't tell me a thing.'

'Your grandfather asked her not to,' her father informed her, adding dryly, 'I guess he thinks that between the two of you, you and Sam have done enough meddling and caused enough potential harm.'

Bobbie hung her head a little as she heard the note of censure in her father's voice.

'Okay,' her father agreed. 'Sam and I will fill you in on what's been happening, but let me go grab a cup of coffee first.'

'We'll wait here,' Samantha said as she fell into step beside her twin and they both followed their father across the concourse. 'And you,' she told Bobbie wickedly, 'can explain to me just how you came to be incommunicado for so long.'

'Later, Sam,' Bobbie hissed, shooting her a warning look, her feelings, her love for Luke and his misconception about her, his lack of love for her, were things she could only discuss with her twin and even then...

She frowned as she realised that for the first time in her life she was experiencing something she didn't want to automatically share with Sam. Something that was so personal that she... Now wasn't the time to start thinking about Luke or last night....

'I still haven't a clue about what's been happening,' Bobbie reminded her father as he returned with the coffee.

'Well, I think we're all still in somewhat of a state of shock,' her father began, 'especially your mother and your grandfather. Seems like we got it wrong all along. Ruth never did want to give up her baby. She felt forced to do so because she knew that her father would never allow her to keep it—he didn't even know she was pregnant. Her mother had guessed and sent her on an extended visit to some distant relatives on her own side of the family, which was why your mother was born in the North-East.'

'Yes, and Grandmother never really stopped loving Grandpa at all,' Samantha chimed in. 'She was told by her father that he was already married with a young child, and because of that, she felt that she had to give him up. It was only after she had sent him away that she found out she was pregnant herself, but she says that even if she had known before, it wouldn't have made any difference because in those days people just didn't divorce the way they do now, and anyway, she could never have lived with herself knowing she had broken up another woman's marriage and deprived her child of its father.'

'Sam, let's start at the beginning,' her father intervened, seeing Bobbie's confusion.

'That was the beginning,' Samantha protested. 'Mom's beginning anyway. Oh...okay,' she relented when she saw the look her father and sister were giving her, 'have it your own way.'

'When I realised that you were in Cheshire,' her father told Bobbie, 'I guessed what the pair of you were most likely up to. I know, of course, how you both feel about your mom, but I was concerned that you might act just a mite too hotheaded and get yourselves into a situation that... Well, in the end I decided I owed it to your grandfather to tell him what was going on.'

'Yes, and then Grandpa came around making a big fuss and insisting that I give him your number in Cheshire.' Samantha scowled. 'I told him I couldn't do that, but you know how he can be.'

Stephen Miller picked up the story again. 'Your grandfather rang Queensmead, Sam having gotten the number from Olivia's answering machine and when she had rung there to try to contact you, Olivia answered the phone and told him that you had already left. She asked him how your mom was and told him how anxious you were about her. It was while they were chatting that your grandfather heard her say, "Oh, Ruth...it's Bobbie's grandfather on the phone enquiring for her, but she's already left."'

'Yes, and that was when Grandpa decided—'

'Thank you, Sam, *I'm* the one telling the story now, remember?' their father warned his daughter dryly as Samantha subsided back into her seat, having given Bobbie a speaking look.

'Well, when your grandfather realised that Ruth was in the same room as Olivia, he decided to do what he says is one of the scariest things he's ever done. He decided that rather than wait until he could get hold of you and talk some sense into you, now that he knew what Sam had in mind for you to do, he owed it to Ruth to at least warn her about what was likely to happen.'

'I'd already decided not to confront her,' Bobbie apprised her father uneasily, giving Samantha an apologetic look as she admitted, 'I just couldn't do it, Sam. I...I liked her too much and...and it just wouldn't have felt right even though...' She shook her head. 'I just couldn't do it.'

'Your grandfather asked Olivia if she would put Ruth on the phone. I guess she was rather surprised, but she called Ruth over and—'

'I could hardly believe it, but Ruth recognised Grandpa's voice right away,' Samantha interrupted excitedly again. 'And then Ruth, Grandmother, started to cry and Grandpa he was practically in tears, too, and Olivia, she had to take the phone from Ruth, but then she had to put her on again because Grandpa wouldn't speak to anyone else and then—'

'Samantha...' her father warned sternly before turning back to Bobbie and continuing, 'Ultimately both Ruth and your grandfather realised that what they'd been told all those years ago, that what they'd believed about one another had been complete untruths. Your grandfather had never been married nor even close to it, never mind having a child.'

Their father looked grave and thoughtful.

'Ruth wanted desperately to keep her baby but in

those days…' He shook his head. 'She was told both by the hospital and by her mother's family that she owed it to your mom to sever herself completely from her, and she wasn't allowed to have any contact with her from just after she was born.

'She told us over the phone how for months after your mother's birth she would wake up in the night, distraught to discover that she was no longer pregnant, unable to work out why, until she remembered that she had already given birth and that her baby was gone.'

Bobbie could feel her eyes starting to fill with tears again as the starkness of her father's revelations stirred her emotions, and Sam, too, she could see was close to tears herself.

'What did Mom say when…when she knew…about Ruth, about her mother?' Bobbie whispered.

Her father smiled gently at her.

'Well, you can imagine she was pretty stunned to learn after all these years that far from not wanting her, her mother had, in fact, never stopped missing her or thinking about her. It probably was a bit much for her to take in at first. I left it to your grandfather to tell her, and well, there were some tears and then… Anyway, it was Ruth who took the initiative, phoning your mom to tell her herself just how she felt about her, and that must have broken the ice. After the first half-hour, the pair of them have hardly been off the phone for ten minutes at a time.'

'I can hardly believe how much has happened,' Bobbie told him, shaking her head.

'Mmm…and where were *you* when it was happening?' Samantha questioned her.

'With Luke,' Bobbie replied simply.

'So Olivia said,' Samantha returned, adding, 'I'm dying to get to know her. She sounds great and, of course, I'm even keener to meet your Luke.'

'He's not...' Just in time Bobbie stopped herself from announcing that Luke was not hers and said quietly instead, 'He's busy at the moment.'

Now that she was over the first shock of learning everything that had happened and despite her happiness for her mother, she was miserably aware that sooner rather than later she was going to have to tell her family just what the real situation was with Luke. Sooner because the last thing she wanted was the embarrassment of their falling on him *en masse* and greeting him as some kind of prospective, soon-to-be family member as they obviously seemed to think he was going to be.

'What's wrong?'

Bobbie and Samantha were sitting in their double room of the hotel suite the family had taken over at the airport hotel. Their parents were having dinner with Jon and Jenny whilst their grandfather had admitted that he was taking Ruth out to dinner—alone.

'We've got a lot of catching up to do,' Grant had informed them when Samantha had raised her eyebrows.

'Sounds like Bobbie's isn't the only romance that's likely to be going on around here,' Samantha had said, adding wryly, 'I'm beginning to feel a little out of place as the only one without a partner.'

Somehow or other Bobbie had managed to force herself to smile.

'Roberta...' Samantha warned.

'It's Luke,' Bobbie admitted, unable to keep her feelings to herself any longer.

'You've had a fight,' Samantha pounced.

Bobbie shook her head. 'It isn't as simple as that,' she told her sister, then went on to briefly outline what had happened.

'He thought what?' Samantha yelped in furious anger when Bobbie got to the part where Luke had accused her of wanting to blackmail Ruth. 'My word, but that's so untrue it's almost funny,' she declared hotly. 'When I think of all the hard times we had as kids persuading Dad and Mom, yes and Grandpa, too, that we weren't going to be turned into a couple of freaks surrounded by bodyguards and so overprotected that we wouldn't know what it was like to live in the real world. When I think of the problems that our family's having serious money has caused for *us*... Did you tell him that far from wanting to blackmail anyone, the pair of us, but you more especially, have spent your grown-up years afraid to let yourself trust any man too much just in case he turns out to be more interested in getting his hands on your money rather than your body? Boy, is he going to have some crawling to do when he finds out the truth,' Samantha asserted in evident satisfaction.

Bobbie permitted herself a sad smile.

'No, Sam,' she said, 'it isn't going to be like that. Luke...well...apart from the fact that he doesn't...that he... He might want me, but he doesn't love me,' she owned painfully. 'And he's the kind of man...well, I just know that his pride will make it impossible for him to admit how badly he's misjudged us...me and my pride. I can't face him again, Sam, not after all that's happened, not now that he knows how I feel about him. I just wish...' She paused. 'If only everyone wasn't so convinced that we're already a couple, then I could just disappear back home and lick my wounds in private...try to forget him.' She frowned suddenly and then announced, 'Sam, I want you to do something for me.'

'No,' Samantha told her firmly.

'I haven't told you what it is yet,' Bobbie complained.

'I don't care. I can tell just by looking at you...just by listening to you, that I'm not going to like it,' Samantha insisted.

'It isn't anything very hard,' Bobbie coaxed her. 'Nothing that I wouldn't do for you....'

Samantha was watching her suspiciously.

Bobbie took a deep breath. 'I want you to pretend to be me,' she told her twin.

Samantha stared at her.

'What...? But the family—'

'No, not to them,' Bobbie corrected her impatiently, 'to Luke. I want you to go and see him and tell him that you hate him and that you never want to see him again.'

Samantha whistled softly and then said, 'Wow!'

'You can be as horrible as you like,' Bobbie encouraged her. 'In fact, the more horrible the better. I want you to make him feel that any idea he had that I might ever have wanted him or felt anything for him, was the *wrong* idea. In fact, I want you to make him thoroughly dislike me so much so that...that in future he isn't even going to want to *speak* to me, never mind anything else.'

'You've got it that bad, huh?' her sister enquired with loving sympathy.

'It's the only way I can stop myself from weakening and...and hoping...perhaps even making a complete fool of myself by...' Bobbie closed her eyes for a moment. 'I love him so much,' she whispered huskily, 'that I'm afraid of what I might do if I have to be around him for too long. This way... I'm going to tell everyone that we've had a fight and that...that I've decided to go home.'

'They won't like that. They're planning to stay here a month and maybe more,' Samantha warned her sister.

'They'll accept it, especially if...well, Mom will understand if she knows I'm hurting and she'll talk to Dad and Grandpa. And then when I'm gone...'

'You want me to go see this Luke and pretend to be you,' Samantha finished for her.

'You will do it, won't you?' Bobbie appealed to her sister.

'What else are twin sisters for?' Samantha responded gruffly.

Bobbie flung herself into her arms and they hugged one another tightly.

CHAPTER EIGHT

SAMANTHA had teased her unmercifully when Bobbie had explained to her what she planned to do with the bathroom of the small house she had bought herself, not with any family money, but with her own earnings.

'You want to what?' she had asked, laughing. 'Oh boy, is that some give-away,' she had teased her sister when Bobbie had reluctantly admitted that the mirrors that had just been delivered were not to go on the front of her wardrobes but were, in fact, to be fitted around her bathroom with one special antique one to hang over the large Victorian footed pedestal bath she had found in a reclamation yard.

And even when the bathroom had finally been finished, Samantha had still shaken her head. 'Well, I guess it does look kinda…interesting,' she had conceded, eyeing the antique filigree candle sconces that decorated the walls and the complementary bronze candle holders that stood on every available surface. 'But are you sure it's a good idea…bathing by candlelight? Won't that make it hard for you to see the dirt?' she had teased and then gone on about the tub. 'Why, I guess two people could quite easily fit in it,' she had mocked innocently whilst Bobbie had given her a murderous look.

So far, though, it had only been put to a solitary and far more mundane use than she had had in mind when she had given in to her romantic and highly sensual yearning for a special place where she and her lover, her *beloved*, could hide themselves away to indulge themselves in the kind of lovemaking that had always been her secret fantasy.

'Identical, huh, that's all they know,' Samantha had scoffed when she had finally teased out of her twin the erotic fantasy behind her plans for her bathroom. 'Personally, *my* choice would be for...' She had paused and then an unfamiliarly dreamy and half-embarrassed look had crossed her face as she admitted, '*My* favourite sensual fantasy would be to make love in some hidden woodland glen with the sound of water somewhere nearby, a stream or preferably a river. It would be springtime—'

'And the squirrels would pelt you with twigs and leaves for invading their privacy, and as for the brown bears...' Bobbie had rolled her eyes expressively and both of them had ended laughing ruefully.

'At least we share a common thing about water, though, I suppose,' Samantha had concluded slyly when they had finally stopped giggling.

'Perhaps...'

But it seemed that she was definitely destined to occupy her own private fantasy retreat on her own, Bobbie acknowledged as she walked tiredly upstairs, heading in the direction of her bathroom.

She had arrived home three days earlier and since then she had been working flat out, dealing with her accumulated backlog of mail, doing some basic shopping, cleaning the house and, in short, doing anything and everything that would keep her mind off Haslewich and Luke.

By now, of course, Sam was bound to have seen him and put their plan into action. He would know then just how wrong he had been about her, about *them*, and being the kind of man he was, she knew that his wretched sense of justice and fair play would not allow him to rest until he made whatever he considered to be due recompense to her for having misjudged her. She knew, too, oh how she knew, that she simply could not bear to

endure his remote kindness and remorse, his pity when
he knew, when they both knew, just how much more
she truly wanted from him.

No, kind and gentle though he might be, it would
carry the same degree of intense pain as the merest
breath against badly burned or other sensitive skin.

Whilst she could withstand his anger and contempt,
his savage condemnation of her by whipping up an answering form of protective anger, she had no defences
against this compassion, which was why she had asked
Sam to change places with her, to be her and to tell him
when he made his apology that it was a little too late,
that there were no amends he could make or that she
wanted him to make; that it had been amusing for a
while to play teasingly with the notion of allowing the
sexual chemistry between them to have its head, but now
she was bored, ready to move on to fresher pastures.

Oh yes, she could see it now, she acknowledged wea-
rily as she shrugged off her clothes and padded naked
from her bedroom to the bathroom, dimming the lights
and slowly, as though it was a ritual, starting to light the
candles she had set here and there around the bath and
on the small occasional tables with the antique lace
cloths. Sam would shake her head and stand her ground,
she would smile ferally at Luke and laugh negligently
as she dismissed her own emotions and him, and when
she had finished there would be, could be, no turning
back because Sam would carry out the role with relish
and inspiration. She would know just how to walk the
fine line that barely separated a woman being free-
spirited from one who was vulgar, a woman who was
hedonistically sensual from one who was brazenly too
sexual.

The candles had a delicate floral fragrance that
warmed the senses and Bobbie breathed it in apprecia-

tively. She was not going to cry, she told herself firmly as she ran herself a bath. There was after all, no need.

It was sad, of course, that Luke did not love her, but one day… She bit down hard on her bottom lip as she fought the pain that sliced through her. A small handful of crystals added to the bath-water turned it a soft shade of blue. In the candlelight, the antique mirrors gave her back her own reflection; her skin looked peachy gold, sun-warmed and ripened, her hair a honey-soft swath that fell silkily below her shoulders, her breasts warm, round globes with deep golden rose nipples, the soft tangle of curls between her legs the same warm honey colour as the hair on her head.

She looked…she looked like a woman who was ready to make love, Bobbie admitted achingly, gently tracing the soft swell of one breast until her fingers started to tremble so much that she had to stop.

Fighting back the tears, she stepped into the bath and then lay back in it, positioning her head on the strategically placed bath pillow and closing her eyes.

The tape she had switched on as she walked into the bathroom was playing Vivaldi, haunting and evocative. One tear escaped from beneath her closed eyelids and then another as her mouth started to quiver.

Cocooned in her private sanctuary, absorbed in her deep sense of loss and pain, she didn't hear the front porch door being unlocked. She didn't even hear the determined swift feet on her stairs as their owner followed the sound of the music.

It was not Bobbie's practice to bolt her bathroom door. Why should she? She lived alone after all. She still had her eyes closed when it was pushed open and it was only the audible swiftness of her visitor's quickly indrawn breath that alerted her to the fact that she was no longer alone.

Galvanised into action she opened her eyes; at the

same time she stood up, starting to reach for a towel, and then froze, shock and disbelief warring for prominence as she stared into Luke's eyes.

'Luke! What are you doing here? How did you...?'

'What the hell do you think I'm doing here?' he muttered thickly and then before she could stop him he was lifting her out of the bath, ignoring both her cries of protest and the damage her soaking wet body had to be doing to his suit, ignoring everything but the need to satisfy the famished need of his mouth to be in the closest possible physical contact with hers.

This wasn't kissing, Bobbie thought incoherently, it was...it was hunger, starvation, wholehearted possession. She could feel herself reacting to his nearness, her whole body starting to tremble, to ache...to burn, with such a searing need that she could no more have denied it than she could have stopped breathing.

She wasn't sure which one of them undressed Luke; she only knew that the sight, the scent, the feel of his naked body, his skin, his flesh against her own, sent such a fierce surge of sensation through her that she was almost too self-consciously embarrassed to meet his eyes.

But far from being shocked, or even worse, contemptuous, of her body's very obvious open, aching need for him, Luke tightened his hold on her and told her hoarsely, 'It's all right...it's all right. I feel exactly the same. God, but I want you...I want you so damn much' that...'

He had started to kiss her again, not just on her mouth this time, but on her throat, her breasts and then her belly. He dragged his mouth against her skin, causing her to shudder violently and moan his name as she pressed herself eagerly against him.

They made love then and there on her bathroom floor, Luke's possessive and open need to fill her with the fiercely powerful stroke of his body matching her own equally strong desire to have him there. Obeying instincts she had never before experienced, Bobbie wrapped her legs tightly around him, holding him securely within her body, keeping him there as she cried out her famished need to him, urging him to possess her totally and completely, so intimately and deeply, that her body would carry the memory of him within it for ever.

Their desire for one another was uncontrollable, a wild, untameable primitive force, their lovemaking quickly reaching its natural climax, and as she felt the hot spurt of Luke's seed deep inside her body, Bobbie knew with some dreamy, illogical female instinct that she would conceive, *had* conceived his child, and that knowledge made her eyes fill with tears of joy, the most exquisite sensation of complete fulfilment engulfing her.

Wonderingly she reached out and touched Luke's face, her eyes darkening as she held his head. He gently kissed the palm of her hand. 'We need to talk,' he told her quietly.

But Bobbie shook her head and closed her eyes defensively, whispering, 'No.'

She was afraid to hear what he might be going to say...or discover why he was even here; she was afraid, too, that now that their hungry desire for one another had been slaked, he would...

'Yes,' Luke insisted, overriding her thoughts, overriding her denial, and asked her quietly, 'Why didn't you tell me the truth?'

'I didn't think you'd believe me,' Bobbie answered huskily.

'Oh, Bobbie...'

She had to swallow hard when she looked at him and saw that his eyes were full of tears.

'What are you doing here anyway?' she asked him shakily. 'I thought that by now Sam would have said enough to ensure that…that you had every reason to hate me.'

He smiled at her and gave her a wry look. 'Nothing and no one could ever do that. Not even you and most certainly not your twin sister. You didn't *really* think I wouldn't *know* she wasn't you, did you?' he asked her roughly as he bent his head and slowly started to caress her exposed nipple, lapping at it with his tongue and then slowly starting to suck on it so that she wriggled protestingly against him.

'How can I concentrate when you're doing that,' she demanded huskily, 'and how did you know that Sam wasn't me? Even our own family can be fooled when we really want to.'

'How do you think I knew?' Luke asked her, and then when she looked questioningly at him, he told her dryly, 'You have a very specific physical effect on my body, to the extent that it can be extremely uncomfortable, not to mention potentially embarrassing being in the same room with you, whereas Samantha…'

'Samantha…?' Bobbie pressed, holding her breath as she lifted her head to look into his eyes.

'Your sister,' Luke told her firmly, 'does not. Yes, physically you may *look* alike, but my body *knows* that you are not. My senses, my emotions, my…my *self* knows you are not. My self knows, for instance, that there is only one Bobbie, only one woman who can make me feel the way she makes me feel, make me ache the way she makes me ache…make me…'

'Mmm…' Bobbie gave a little moan as Luke interspersed his words with increasingly lingering kisses.

His hand cupped her body, holding the soft, still-damp tangle of pubic curls; he caressed her gently and felt her body shudder in delighted response.

'We shouldn't really be doing this,' he murmured. 'I was in such a damned hurry to see you that the thought of doing anything about precautions never even crossed my mind.'

'If I'm right in what I'm thinking, I'm pretty sure that it's too late to start worrying about that now anyway,' Bobbie told him with shy breathlessness.

The look in his eyes as he translated her muddled words drove away any lingering doubts she might have felt the need to cling protectively to and any pretence that she didn't love him.

'You mean you think...' He paused and took a deep breath, his nostrils flaring. 'Already...?'

'Already,' Bobbie whispered back.

'If you're right, that just shows how good we are together, how right for one another,' Luke told her lovingly. His hand still covered her body and Bobbie moved slightly against it, conscious of the ache already building inside her again.

This time their lovemaking was far more leisurely. In the candlelight, Bobbie watched their mirror reflections as Luke slowly and thoroughly kissed every single inch of her. They could have been two Renaissance lovers in some romantic Venetian *palazzo*. There was something almost wickedly and alluringly sensual about the way their bodies moved together, fitted together.... Bobbie gave a voluptuous, shuddering sigh of pleasure as Luke's mouth reached the place where his hand had been.

'So when did you first know you loved me?' Luke demanded half an hour later as they sat at Bobbie's breakfast bar, wrapped in thick, fluffy towelling robes, Bobbie watching whilst Luke cooked her some scrambled eggs.

'I knew there was something very special and very dangerous going on the first time you kissed me,' Bobbie admitted, watching his face as she asked, 'and you...?'

'Oh, long, long before that.' He started to laugh, and then stopped laughing as he told her soberly, 'I fell in love with you as soon as I set eyes on you, but I definitely knew it that night at my flat.'

'I couldn't believe you'd left me there alone and free to "escape",' Bobbie interjected.

'I needed time to think, to come to terms with the reality of my love for you, and perhaps psychologically, I wanted you to go, but I wanted to keep you, as well— for ever!'

'How did you know I'd be here, that I'd even want to see you after all the things you'd said and done...and how did you manage to get in?' Bobbie asked Luke curiously once she had finally started to come back down to earth.

Luke's admission that he had fallen in love with her on sight had resulted in the scrambled eggs he had just cooked for her being left to grow cold whilst she showed him just how she felt about it.

The rueful look Luke was giving her now made her gasp in indignation, 'Samantha told you,' she guessed, using her twin's full name as an indication of how seriously she viewed this departure from sisterly solidarity.

'Yes, but only after she had persuaded me to tell her how I felt about you,' Luke assured her. 'Until she knew that, I can tell you she was pretty fearsome in her desire to let me know what kind of a rat she thought me and pretty resourceful in her attempts to prevent me from guessing just how you felt and where you were, despite the fact that I'd already warned her that I knew she wasn't you.

'She doesn't kiss anything like you,' he whispered teasingly and then reached out and wrapped Bobbie tightly in his arms as he saw the look in her eyes, holding her firmly as he whispered, 'Hey, come on, do you think I wanted to kiss her, or indeed kiss anyone but you, and even if I had wanted to, do you think she would have let me?'

'I never suspected I could be this jealous.' Bobbie grimaced.

'Me neither,' Luke admitted. 'So jealous in fact that right now I hate the thought of ever having to share you with anyone else, even your twin.'

'And our baby?' Bobbie asked.

'We'll get married just as soon as it can be arranged,' Luke told her masterfully and then gave her a wry look as he asked penitently, 'You do *want* to marry me, don't you, Bobbie?'

'Yes,' she agreed softly. 'Whether or not a couple decide to marry is a very personal decision and one only they can make, but I guess after seeing the effect that not knowing her mother had on my mom, I feel that I want to make it as difficult as possible for either of us to ever walk away from our children.'

'Children, is it now?' Luke teased, his mouth against hers. 'You know what that means, don't you...?'

'What?' Bobbie asked, her question muffled by his kiss.

'Let's go back upstairs and I'll show you,' Luke suggested wickedly.

EPILOGUE

Five months later

'TRUST you,' Samantha moaned to Bobbie as they tried on their matching dresses. 'I just get to be Gran's bridesmaid, while you have to go and be her matron of honour, a very blooming matron of honour, as well,' she added meaningly, glancing at the small swell discreetly covered by the high-waisted style of their long dresses. 'You know there's going to be one heck of a lot of finger counting by the family back home when Junior arrives.'

When Bobbie laughed, Samantha watched her in fascination.

'You just don't care, do you?' she marvelled. 'And to think that you've always been considered the conservative one. If that's what being in love does for you, I guess I'd better not try it.'

'You should,' Bobbie told her twin vigorously. 'I can definitely recommend it.'

Samantha rolled her eyes. 'I think two romances and two weddings in the family within nearly as many months is sufficient, don't you?' she asked her sister tartly.

Bobbie smiled. 'I think it's wonderful that Grandpa and Ruth have actually decided to get married,' she told her sister dreamily. 'I mean, I know it was obvious how they felt about one another. Luke laughed when he brought me back to England. He said that watching the two of them together made him feel positively inhibited and old-fashioned....'

Samantha rolled her eyes again. 'He certainly wasn't inhibited in private, was he?' she reminded her twin dryly.

Bobbie laughed again.

'Who'd have thought twelve months ago that within a year one of us would have actually married one of the enemy and become a Crighton? And even more incredible, that Ruth and Grandpa should have fallen in love with one another all over again and if it hadn't been for the coincidence of Ruth happening to be there when Grandpa telephoned Queensmead to speak to you...?'

'I don't think they ever fell out of love with one another,' Bobbie responded soberly, 'and as for coincidence, Grandpa claims it's like twins and that it runs in families!'

They both laughed.

'Yes, and Mom is so loving it, isn't she? I've never seen her so happy.'

'No, me neither,' Samantha agreed, declaring triumphantly, 'You see, our plan worked after all....'

'*Our* plan?' Bobbie questioned drolly and then reached out to hug her twin. 'Oh, I do hope you find someone soon, Sam. Junior in here is going to want to have cousins to play with, you know,' she warned her sister as she patted her stomach.

'I don't *need* a man to provide him or her with that, not these days,' Samantha retaliated, adding ruminatively, 'In fact, I rather think that might be a good idea. I could—'

'Sam!' Bobbie warned her twin. '*Whatever* it is you're planning, the answer is *no. No...no* again. Now, come on, let's get these dresses on properly. The rehearsal for the wedding starts in half an hour and we're going to be late. Luke will be here to pick us up and we won't be ready unless we hurry....'

As she quickly finished fastening her matron-of-honour gown, she studied her twin uneasily. Samantha wouldn't do anything so foolish as she had just suggested...would she? Would she! No! No, of course she wouldn't.

Continue to thrill to the pleasures and frustrations, heartaches and passions of the Crighton family with Saul's story.
Saul Crighton is every woman's dream— sexy, charming and a devoted single father to three children. Everyone agrees that he's perfect marriage material. Everyone, that is, except Tullah...
Read on for a tantalising extract from Penny Jordan's next book to feature the fascinating Crighton family:

PERFECT MARRIAGE MATERIAL

'NIGHT night, Daddy,' Meg murmured drowsily, lifting her head from her pillow to kiss Saul as he bent over her, and then to Tullah's consternation she added, 'I want Tullah to kiss me, as well.'

Uncomfortably Tullah edged carefully round Saul as he turned towards Robert's bed.

'Night night, Tullah. Thank you for reading to us,' Meg told her lovingly as Tullah kissed her gently.

She could feel Saul standing behind her, feel him almost as though their bodies, their skins, were actually touching. Her face flamed at the treacherous direction her thoughts were taking. Not that they had any reason to do so, she decided crossly five minutes later as she started back downstairs.

And she couldn't even begin to think why her heart suddenly wanted to audition for a circus act and turn spectacularly dizzying and breathtaking somersaults. It was impossible that such an unfamiliar reaction could have been caused by Saul's proximity. Impossible, unpalatable and completely untenable, she decided firmly and then gasped aloud as her foot missed one of Olivia's uneven stairs and she started to fall forward.

Instinctively she cried out, but Saul was already reaching for her and responding to her plight, quickly grasping hold of and virtually swinging Tullah off her feet and back against his body as he caught her in mid fall.

Shaken and breathless, Tullah could only cling weakly to him as she later wrathfully mentally berated herself like a second-rate actress trying for a part in *Gone with the Wind*. Only she was no dainty, fragile lightweight, but a healthy, modern young woman who prided herself on keeping her rebelliously feminine curves under control with thrice-weekly gym workouts and as many fresh-air walks as she could fit into her busy schedule.

But if the effect of supporting her, *holding* her, wrapped in his arms against his chest, was imposing any kind of physical strain on him, Saul certainly wasn't showing it, Tullah acknowledged.

Yes, his heartbeat *had* accelerated. His muscles had tightened as he tautly braced himself against her weight, but from her snugly secure position against his body with her head tucked protectively into the oh so comfortable space between his shoulder and his jaw that might have been made for her, she could neither see nor feel any evidence of his straining.

'I...I...you can put me down now,' Tullah started to inform Saul in what she had intended to be a courteous but dismissively distant tone. But what emerged instead sounded revolting, coy and horribly breathless.

'That's just as well, because I'm afraid my endurance and stamina are just about to give in. They aren't really up to much more,' Saul told her dryly.

Feeling mortified, Tullah immediately started to push herself away from him as he carefully set her back down on her own feet. It was perhaps unfair of her to feel that he was being ungallant in announcing that he found her too heavy but she was, after all, a woman and as such surely allowed to be a little illogical if and when she wished.

'I'm sorry if I'm too heavy,' she apologised insincerely once she was back on the floor and able to take a couple of wary steps away from him as she moved a little bit farther downstairs but this time concentrating on where she was putting her feet and holding on to the stair rail in addition.

'I never said you were too heavy,' Saul murmured to her before leaning forward and almost absently straightening the rucked collar of her top.

Tullah gaped at him, too caught off guard by the unconscious intimacy of his careful, almost paternal touch, the kind of touch she could so easily imagine him giving to one of his children, to think to question his words very deeply. If he wanted to backtrack and pretend that he hadn't implied she was too heavy...

His hand was still resting on her shoulder, his fingertips touching the bare flesh of her collarbone.

Upstairs, the children had fallen silent. They were completely alone in the still intimacy of the narrow stairway.